Closing the Book on Santa Claus & Other Holiday Stories

By

Ron Chandler

(Edited by Mia R. Cortez)

Table of Contents

Slickest Road Ever

It was the coldest Christmas Eve ever. So cold that pedestrians wrapped scarves over their mouths to keep teeth from chattering and stuffed their hands into gloves to keep frostbite from turning fingertips blue. Normally, if the temperature hovered in the low 40s that would be cold, but every thermometer registered eight degrees or below, which made Baltimore colder than Yukon, Alaska by the Arctic Circle. And all the dangers of the frozen North were carried a thousand miles south to an unsuspecting city.

The furnaces in the Oak Grove Apartments were at least 50 years old and rattled and hissed, but the air they blew out kept the residents' apartments warm. Brenda was glad of that. She was nine months, three days pregnant and couldn't imagine what would happen if the heat gave out. The doctor told her *If your pregnancy lasts another two weeks, I'll induce labor.* She couldn't imagine carrying this child for another two seconds much less two whole weeks. She flopped onto the sofa and looked outside, wishing her husband was home and could run to the store to buy some sea salt. That was her latest craving. She had been through all of them: quarts of rocky road ice cream, bags of barbeque-flavored potato chips, boxes of chocolate-covered honey-dips, gallons of cranberry juice, pounds of deep-fried lake trout. Now it was sea salt. She would sprinkle it on a peanut butter and jelly sandwich, dissolve a pinch or two in a cup of tea, or spoon it into a bowl of cereal.

A rapping sound came from the front door. When she opened it, Garth stood there with cowlicks spiking his black hair and his lanky arms and body resembling a scarecrow. He had moved to Baltimore six months ago from western Maryland and gotten a job at Lexington Market to learn how to sell the vegetables his family grew on their farm back home. Originally, he intended to be in town for only a week or two, but Garth was not the quickest thinker. It took him a year to learn how to milk a cow and all he had to do was connect the suction cups to their udders. It took him another two to learn how to do it by hand. But that didn't mean God had no sympathy for him. God likes super-smart people. He lets them acquire great wealth and fame and often a butler and maid. God is fond of average people. He knows they have marital problems and get headaches from paying bills and ulcers from their trouble-loving teenagers so He gave them The Book for guidance. However, God loves people that are slow thinkers. You can tell that because most of them have no worries. Their only concern is making it through the day. And they have a blind faith that gets them into heaven quicker than a greased pig sliding through someone's hands. Garth gave her several letters as he said in his country drawl, "Ms. McLean, they done put your mail in my box."

"Thanks. Could you be an angel and go to the shopping mall for me?" She pressed a 20 dollar bill into his palm and said, "Please pick up a ten-pound bag of Baltic Sea Salt."

"Ten pounds of salt?" His eyelids blinked rapidly over his pale blue eyes as though he had trouble understanding the request.

"Yes, Baltic Sea Salt. It's my latest craving."

"Okay, Ms. McLean. I'll be back in a jiffy."

He strolled toward the shopping center which was in a neighborhood called Northwood although nobody could ever find enough trees to make up a *wood* since there was only one oak or sycamore per block. Snowflakes floated down in a swirling motion and were whisked back up again and glided back as softly as white parachutes. In less than a minute a film coated the grass plots in the median strip of Loch Raven Boulevard. In 15 minutes a layer stuck to the street and sidewalk, but it was easy to walk through because it was so light. In fact, it was the fluffiest snow ever.

Ammonia reeked from the floor in the Stop'n'Shop and the lights overhead shined so bright that Garth wished he was sporting sunglasses. He saw *spices* listed on the aisle 5 directory and found that section, but the store only carried five pound-containers of Morton's Salt. "Where can I find Baltic Sea Salt?" he asked a clerk stocking canned goods.

"We don't carry that crap," the man snorted. "Go down to the health food store."

Garth strode toward the other end of the strip mall. There was a man, dressed in black pants and a black overcoat, standing next to a black kettle and ringing a large bell. He yodeled, "Help the poor. Salvation Army drive."

Garth pulled a dollar out of his pocket and slipped it into the kettle.

"Thank you, sir. Have a happy holiday."

When Garth opened the door to Mother Nature's Cupboard, he heard the jingle of bells and smelled the musky odor of organic vegetables grown in soil fertilized by cow dung. He glided past bottles of vitamins and minerals from A to Zinc, New Age cookbooks penned by vegetarian gurus, loaves of fresh baked bread ranging from whole wheat to rice to eight-grain, and an assortment of exotic herbs such as ginseng, kava root, St. John's wort, palmetto berry, and olive leaf. Then he saw it: Baltic Sea Salt in ten pound bags. The salt was an ugly gray color. He couldn't understand why anyone would want to buy it, but he was running an errand for a lady so pregnant she looked as though she had swallowed a watermelon. When he first met her, Ms. McLean looked like any other stylish blonde living in the city. As the baby got bigger, she let herself go. She didn't dye her hair and now had black roots an inch long. Her butt sagged from the weight she had gained and her face became chubby. And recently dark bags had formed underneath her eyes from the baby *kicking her awake at night.* But she was still one of the sweetest women ever.

The cashier's ponytail swished like a horse's tail as he asked, "Do you want a plastic bag for that?"

"Sure."

"They're right over there."

Garth bagged the salt and carried it outside. There were now a couple women wearing dark dresses standing beside the Salvation Army man. It made him homesick looking at them because they reminded him of his Mennonite neighbors in western Maryland. They all had open books in their hands and were caroling:

Hark the herald angels sing
"Glory to the newborn King!
Peace on earth and mercy mild
God and sinners reconciled"
Joyful, all ye nations rise…

He was enjoying the moment, then stepped out from underneath the sidewalk canopy.

Freezing rain pelted his face. A warm front from the south was rising over the cold front. Rain passed through a layer of frigid air close to the ground and hardened into silver bullets that tinkled on the sidewalk and street. Garth slid on a slick spot, but maintained his balance. He crouched down, stuck out his arms, and tiptoed the quarter mile back to the apartments as though he was on a tightrope. He grabbed the handrail to climb the building's cement steps. He entered the foyer and banged on Brenda's door.

"Back already?"

"Yes, ma'am." He handed her the bag.

"You're a life saver, Garth. There's nothing better than Baltic Sea Salt." She ripped the bag open and shoveled two teaspoons into her orange juice. "It contains over 75 minerals: chloride, sodium, sulfur, magnesium, potassium, calcium, silicon, carbon, iron…" She stirred her drink and took a sip. "Mmm, this is the best orange juice ever…aluminum, praseodymium, strontium, zinc, copper, erbium, tin… Would you like to try it?" She tipped her glass toward him.

"No, ma'am, I'll take your word for it," he said, then galloped upstairs to his apartment.

Brenda returned to her living room. She had no intention of going anywhere. The rain was playing a tune on the roof and icicles hung off storm drains. She felt cozy sitting on the sofa watching daytime dramas, but her baby had other ideas because her water broke like the Grand Coulee Dam bursting open and unleashing the Columbia River.

She phoned Garth. What choice did she have? Her husband worked downtown and couldn't get there.

Garth hustled downstairs and knocked.

She opened the door. "It's time. I've called a cab. Please help me with my suitcase."

Garth picked it up and waited.

She felt a trickling sensation down her leg. Her doctor said the *amniotic fluid* might continue to drip until childbirth. Her womb was a ticking time bomb with the baby about to pop out. She grabbed the bag of Baltic Sea Salt and waddled toward her escort.

He closed the door and followed her outside.

A yellow cab was waiting for them with its engine humming. The driver had oily black hair, a stocky build, and tan complexion. He jumped out of the driver's seat and yodeled, "Momma Mia, you got a stuffed ravioli there."

"This is my next door neighbor, Brenda," said Garth.

"I'm a'Dominick. Let me help you, Lady."

"Get me to Union Memorial right now!" she demanded.

They loaded her suitcase into the trunk and eased her into the back seat. Garth was just about to close the door when she shrieked, "Aren't you coming with me?"

"No, I'm going back to my apartment."

"You can't leave me alone!" Brenda tugged on his coat collar. "My husband isn't here. You have to be my Bradley in case the baby comes." She had chosen the husband-coached Bradley Method to give birth and now she had to settle for him, but what other options did she have? She had only known Dominick for a minute.

"Okay, Ms. McLean, you talked me into it." That was the biggest endorsement Garth had received from a woman ever. Most ignored him as though he wasn't even there. He climbed in.

The cab rolled down the hill to Loch Raven Boulevard, but skidded on a patch of snow. One moment it was doing a wheelie to the left and the next, to the right. They could have been on a carnival ride. The whole time Dominick chatted about the weather and the other fares he had that day at such a fast pace the meter must have been running on his mouth.

"Oh!" Brenda huffed. "I feel a contraction."

"Drive faster, Dominick."

"I'm a'trying." The cabbie cupped a silver medallion in his hand. It dangled from the rearview mirror and was engraved with the figure of an old man holding a staff. The man was fording a stream with the child *Jesus* riding on his back. "By the grace of Saint Christopher we'll get there safely."

By the time they got to 33rd Street, Brenda was caroling in the back seat, "*Oh! Oh! Eee…ooww!*" over and over again.

The wheels spun around a thousand times, but couldn't get any traction. A solid sheet of ice covered this street. The cab slid into the curb. Garth got out and pushed, and an acrid cloud of exhaust puffed in his face. Dominick gunned the motor and the wheels whined, but still the car would not move. They were stuck on the slickest road ever.

Garth had seen this before. In winter whenever he led the cows to the barn for milking, their hooves would plunk through crusty snow and gain firm footing on the ground underneath; but when they reached the slick pavement leading to the stalls, their legs would give out and cause them to slide onto their rumps. The same thing had happened here. The rump of the cab was stuck on the curb.

"I need your sea salt, Ms. McLean," said Garth as he grabbed the bag.

She clutched the other corner and pulled back. Soon they were involved in a gigantic tug-of-war, sliding back and forth in the back seat, rocking the cab from side to side.

"What's going on back there?" yelled Dominick.

"Nothing," said Garth. And to Brenda, "Give me that bag of salt!"

"You're not going anywhere," she growled. Now she was tugging on his coat with both hands. "You're my Bradley. You got to deliver my baby."

Garth had seen calves born, but had no intention seeing Brenda's baby born in the back seat. That was taking neighborliness a bit too far. "Please, Ms. McLean, let me help you the best way I can. Dominick, take my place."

The cabbie's eyes became as large as silver dollars, "I'm a'fine right here."

"The heck you are. Your cab is stuck and this baby is ready to spill out. Get back here."

Dominick scooted outside and opened the back door. When he leaned forward to exchange places with Garth, Ms. Mclean put a strangle hold on both of them.

"Uh!" gasped Dominick.

Garth swam through her hands as she groped for him and bolted free.

The poor cabbie was pulled in and squeezed like a sponge with beads of sweat dotting his brow.

Garth sprinkled Baltic Sea Salt from the grill of the cab all the way to the grass plot in the middle of the road which was now covered with a few inches of snow and ice. He settled into the front seat behind the steering wheel.

"I'm a'coming over." Dominick tried to climb over the rear seat, but was pulled backwards by Ms. McLean and wrestled into submission.

"Don't worry, Dominick. I've driven tractors through knee-deep mud, across shallow streams, even on ice and snow."

"I'm a'praying to Saint Christopher, *Please deliver my darling safely.*" Dominick smooched the seat cushion.

The wheels caught onto something, and they spurted forward. Garth steered the cab toward the grass plot and over the curb. They bounced up and down whenever it hit a bump, and the chassis groaned. He weaved around bushes. He gunned it across intersections where ice glazed the asphalt and rode up onto the next grass plot. All around them vehicles were spinning wheels and going nowhere, a bus plowed into a newspaper box on the corner, and a police cruiser was twirling round and round in the middle of 33rd Street like a children's toy. Then the cab got stuck in a gully, and spun its wheels. Garth lowered the window and hollered, "Hey, kids, can you help us? This here lady is having a baby."

A bunch of kids building a snowman gathered around. "Are you talking about a real baby, mister?"

"As real as one can be."

They pushed on the trunk.

Garth punched the gas pedal with his foot, and the cab sputtered free.

Plunk! Plunk! Plunk! The kids splattered the rear window with snowballs.

When he saw the bright hospital lights, Garth steered in that direction. The cab slid down a driveway and stopped about twenty yards from the Emergency Room. A team of nurses and orderlies helped Ms. McLean inside. The doctor on duty was astonished because even the ambulance crews could not make it in.

Her husband, Rick, was wearing big leather boots and a trench coat. "Hon', are you all right?" he asked. "I've hiked all the way from North Avenue."

Brenda nodded and forced a grin through the contractions.

The baby was born in the maternity ward of Union Memorial Hospital. The parents christened him: William Garth McLean. To them it was the most special Christmas Eve ever.

Closing the Book on Santa Claus

Children marked off the days on the wall calendar as December 2005 rolled on, hoping that this year's winter holiday would be the best. Each year their holiday celebration got bigger as they advanced in grade. Unfortunately, when Jennifer's third grade class returned from gym on Wednesday afternoon, workmen were carting their pine tree out the door. She grabbed onto a branch and pulled back. She whined, "What about our decorations?"

"We put them on the table," said one workman. Silver bells, Styrofoam snowmen, fairies, elves, penguins, polar bears, snowflakes cut-out in intricate shapes, red and white striped candy canes, gingerbread houses, doves, angels, and a gold star of Bethlehem that had glittered on the treetop were heaped there.

The other workman pleaded. "Please let go, miss."

Two boys in her class grabbed onto the tree too. Cones popped off, landing on the floor with a rustling sound, as they played tug-of-war.

"Everyone stop," ordered their teacher. "Please tell me the meaning of this?"

"Ms. Cartwright told us to take the tree," said a workman. "She said if it's not in the school's curriculum, you can't teach it."

"I see," replied their teacher, gritting her teeth. "Jennifer, Brad and Cole, please let go."

They did as their teacher told them. The workmen dragged the tree, which screeched on the hallway floor, toward the dumpster. Children settled in their seats. Their teacher resumed class as if nothing had happened. When the school bells tolled, Jennifer buttoned up her coat. The bus ride home was unusually quiet. The children seemed cold or dumbfounded by what the workmen did. When her dad came home, Jennifer settled on his lap before dinner.

"What's wrong, kitten?" he purred. It was unusual for his daughter to come see him instead of being holed up in her bedroom with her homework. Her brown hair hung forward, covering her cherub face, and her shoulders sagged. "You can tell me."

She unfolded her hand, which held a pine cone. "They took away our tree and the candlestick."

"The Menorah?" asked her dad.

She nodded.

"I'll go down there tomorrow and get to the bottom of this."

When Peter visited the Grandview Academy in the morning, he discovered that his daughter's teacher had been reprimanded for allowing an infraction of school rules. He lodged a complaint at the CEO's office, but was told nothing could be done to restore the children's holiday celebration. Even so the issue leaked out into the neighborhood and after a flurry of charges and countercharges between the Parent Teacher Association (PTA) and the Administration, the issue landed at a public hearing before the board of the most prestigious school in Baltimore City. Its members sat behind a table elevated on a little stage and peered down at the many parents and children seated in the gallery. Barb Cartwright, the CEO of Grandview Academy, was a graceful looking woman with her blonde hair pulled back in a chignon and blue eyes set in a thin, pale face. She spoke bluntly, "Students are enrolled in our school to learn the common core curriculum. They are not here to celebrate religious holidays." She jabbered a while about various state and federal regulations, and asked if there were any questions.

Peter refused to budge. Standing tall, he asked, "What better place is there to teach religious tolerance than in a classroom? I would like to introduce three wise men who support my position."

The first was a minister who had played football in high school, but was now middle-aged with a bald head and potbelly. He wore a pink shirt and spoke softly, "On Christmas we celebrate the birth of our savior. While Santa can bring a little joy to children by giving presents, Jesus possesses the power to save their souls."

The next speaker was a Hassidic rabbi dressed similar to a pilgrim at Plymouth Rock with a wide-brimmed black hat, black pants and shoes, and a starched white shirt framed by a full-length black coat. His bushy gray beard poked the microphone as he spoke, "Hanukkah should be observed along with Christmas. Our holiday celebrates the Maccabees' victory over the armies of the cruel dictator, Antiochus IV, and the restoration of our temple. We commemorate Hanukkah by lighting a menorah."

Then Peter presented an Imam dressed in a long white robe and a white cap. The kids stirred with excitement when they saw him because he reminded them of the ice cream man who drove a van down their streets during the summer months. He had a copper complexion and spoke in a Middle Eastern accent. "Eid al-Fitr marks the end of our month of fasting, Ramadan. We pay homage to Allah by praying and sharing a meal with our relatives and neighbors. It is a time for reconciliation and forgiveness. Please allow this Christmas celebration to take place and honor our Holy days."

When Barb Cartwright stood up again, she sneered. "Children are not in school to play games. We will close the book on Santa Claus. Our school will not be celebrating Kwanza, Christmas, Hanukkah, the Muslim Holy days or any another religious holidays. I guess next you're going to tell me something preposterous like *There is a God.*"

"Jesus," prayed the minister, "please forgive her."

"What type of message are you sending to the next generation?" asked the rabbi.

"Allah will not forgive statements like that," scolded the Imam. "You will burn in the sixth level of hell."

Peter decided to organize a rally to protest the school board's ruling. He went door-to-door in his neighborhood and invited parents and children to attend, talked to the president of the PTA, called the leaders of other neighborhood associations, and contacted Sam Johnson, a reporter for the local newspaper. The next morning he drove over to his brother's house after attending church. To his surprise there was a lot of commotion because his brother and friends were getting ready to go to M & T Stadium to watch the Ravens play. His brother's big belly was covered by the purple jersey of his favorite player Ray Lewis, number 52, a middle linebacker, and his gray hair, which was beginning to turn white, was spiked to look like daggers. A black bird's beak was strapped overtop his nose, his legs were stuffed into black boots shaped to resemble bird's feet with four black claws protruding from the toes, and a necklace made of plastic bones jangled around his neck. From a distance he looked like a cross between a punk rocker and a raven. One of his friends kept blowing a whistle that went *caw caw.* That fellow wore the jersey of Jonathan Ogden, number 75, an offensive tackle, and had purple and black stripes painted on his face. His brother barked, "Hey Pete, we're taking flight."

"Slow down!" yelled Peter, grabbing his younger brother's shirt to keep him from running away. Roger had always been a bit wild, and required a lot of arm twisting to do the right things. "I need a favor."

"Spill it. I don't have time to talk."

"I'm organizing a rally at City Hall next Saturday. We're going to ask the mayor to allow holiday celebrations back in the schools."

"Sure, bro, I'll tell Meg. She'll probably want to go."

"I want you. We need someone to be our Santa Claus."

"I don't know. If people see me dressed up like that, they'll think I'm a weirdo."

"Come on, Roger, help me out."

Meg had come out of the house carrying a jug full of soda and wearing earrings resembling ravens. "He'll do it," she yodeled. "Call back after we stomp on the Steelers and pick their bones clean."

"Yeah, I'll do it."

That afternoon Sam Johnson stopped by Peter's house to ask questions about the rally and a photographer snapped a picture of Peter, and his daughter, Jennifer, hanging up Christmas lights. Little did Peter know that the publicity generated by his actions would seep down to all levels of society.

Joel liked sleeping on the portico of the Roman Catholic Basilica even in winter. He would wrap newspapers around his feet and snuggle up in his coat and drift into dreamland, sometimes imagining he was a playboy in Miami going to the beach with his girlfriends who giggled and squealed whenever they splashed through the waves, and at other times reliving his youth playing baseball and football on vacant lots. When he woke up, he often heard the cheerful chirping of birds. However, on Monday morning the blare of car horns and the squealing of brakes roused him as commuters competed with holiday shoppers for road space. Then he heard Ben, his pal, griping. Ben was an old African-American man who lost his home in New Orleans to Hurricane Katrina and took the bus here to look for work. When Joel first met him, Ben explained, "The gov'ment spen' plenty of money rebuildin' Iraq, but not one penny for this poor man's 'hood. We had floodwater coming up to our eyeballs. Swam through it like fish to get to the Superdome. When we got there, they gave us no food, no water, and no place to take a leak. Wasn't fit for man nor animal. Insects feasted on our waste." Ben had a raspy voice and played the trumpet by the subway station to get spare change though he was not as smooth as his idol, Louie "Satchmo" Armstrong. Sometimes his voice was so gravelly, Joel didn't know if he was speaking or clearing phlegm from his throat. "This here pants has a hole in them," said Ben as he stood nearby with his bare knee poking out.

"Don't worry. We'll go down to the Wards building and get it fixed. Why don't you stuff this in there?" asked Joel, handing him a sheet of newspaper.

Ben folded it into the hole and flexed his leg to make sure the filling wouldn't fall out.

Joel rose, and the two of them began their pilgrimage.

On any given night anywhere from 50 to 100 homeless people gathered in the parking lot behind the abandoned Montgomery Ward building near Carroll Park. They pushed shopping carts or lugged knapsacks loaded with their stuff - old blankets and sleeping bags donated by the Salvation Army, sheets of plastic picked up at construction sites, cardboard boxes dumped behind Lexington Market, and curtains thrown out by roadside motels. At dusk they trekked from various parts of downtown Baltimore and set up their makeshift dwellings in the moonlight or under starshine. Parties often broke out with men sharing bottles of wine or beer, and the last stragglers arrived after 2 a.m. Then everything settled down. When morning came, the sunlight showed the canary, maroon, silver, and lime trimmings of a tent city and commuters driving by on Interstate 95 would look down and think, *Oh! There must be a carnival going on.*

That's where they found Sara. She was a small woman with stringy white hair and a surly manner. When she saw them, she barked, "What you got for me?"

Ben unwrapped a crumpled piece of wax paper and showed her a half-eaten hamburger, its grease dried on the edges.

"I don't eat food from the trash. If you want your pants fixed, bring me something better than that. I like the cake at the Turk's."

They bounded a couple blocks to the bakery whose name was written in a backward looking alphabet above the door. Joel looked through the picture window and saw a thin man about five and a half feet tall with an olive complexion and dark mustache serving hot buns to several women seated at a table. When he walked inside, all types of intoxicating aromas made his mouth water. The shelves were stocked with a wide array of Middle Eastern goods - baklava seasoned with walnuts or pistachios, sweet cookies studded with almonds or raisins, salty cookies with the texture of soft pretzels, rolls covered with sesame seeds, cakes filled with globs of caramel or orange marmalade, and a treat called rahat lokum, more commonly known as Turkish Delight, a sweet made from gelatin and concentrated grape juice and flavored with rosewater or lemon which gave it a pink or yellow color. It has a soft, jelly-like texture and is often cut into bite-sized squares stuffed with nuts and dried fruit. Some were filled with apricot, almond, and honey while others had hazelnut, carrot, and coconut. Turkish Delight was rumored to be an aphrodisiac that transformed weaklings with slumped shoulders into robust male studs with a vigorous appetite for sensual pleasure. Consequently, on any given day more men entered the bakery than women. Joel stood there, dumbfounded for a moment.

The Turk saw a wiry man with curly hair and clothes stained with the grime of city streets. "You look like a traveler, my friend. How may I help you?"

"Give me two slices of the orange cake," requested Joel.

"Of course. Ottah is always glad to make a new customer." He hurried around the counter and lifted two slices with his serving knife onto a paper plate. The cake was coated with orange icing and had globs of orange marmalade inside each tangy slice. He covered it with a clear wrap and said, "That will be $3.25."

Joel slapped a quarter and dime on the counter, and replied, "I'll be back next week to pay you the rest."

When he reached for the plate, Ottah pulled it back. "I am sorry, my friend, these are for customers who pay in full."

"Can't you give me a break?" he begged. "I need the food. It's not for me. It's for Sara. She's going to fix my pal's pants."

"I spend three hours every morning baking my goods in the ovens," explained Ottah. "How do you think I pay for the flour, sugar, and electricity that makes these? I am not a cruel Turk. By the grace of Allah I can offer you this 50 pound bag of flour." He lifted up a huge bag and plopped it on the counter. Then he cruelly teased, "You can bake your own buns if you know how."

"Ah, forget it." The door slapped behind Joel as he left.

They wandered down the street begging strangers for money and got grunts and shrugged shoulders in return. They saw a fellow coming out of the café with his family. "'Scuse me, sir," pleaded Joel, "can you spare fifty cents?"

"I'm sorry." The man, turning to his wife and son, snapped, "Let's go."

"Hon', let's help them," said his wife. "Where's your Christmas spirit?"

"Why should I give them anything?"

"It's not for us," admitted Joel. "It's for Sara."

"Who's Sara?" scolded the man. "A tramp you met last night?"

"Hey, she's a good lady, mister," said Ben. "She's goin' to fix my pants if we get her some food."

"Come on, Hon'," chimed his wife.

"All right." He pulled out his wallet.

"What would *Sara* like to have for breakfast?" she asked.

Joel thought for a moment. "Scrambled eggs, hash browns, and toast."

The man gave his wife a five dollar bill, and she disappeared into the café. He stood there hugging his boy as though he was afraid they would kidnap him. They listened to the snowmelt dripping off the roof and crows cawing from a light pole.

His wife came back out with a brown bag stained with a spot of grease. "Before we give you this, you must promise to pass on the favor to someone else…*in the Christmas spirit.*"

"Yeah, Lady," said Ben, "we'll do that."

"Yes, ma'am," pledged Joel, "I will."

They trotted toward the Montgomery Ward building which had most of its windows busted out. Ben stopped and lifted the bag up and down. "You know this is pretty heavy 'specially for a small woman like Sarah."

Joel picked it up. "Yeah, it is."

Instead of supersizing it, they downsized it. Joel shoveled some hash browns into his mouth with a plastic fork. Ben feasted on the toast. "Hold on!" Joel slapped Ben's hand. "Don't eat it all. Leave some for Sara."

Only half a slice remained when they gave the breakfast to her. She dug into the scrambled eggs and the small mound of hash browns. She picked up the piece of toast and gasped, "What's this?" and looked around in the bottom of the bag for the other half.

"They don't make things the way they used to," said Joel. "Not even breakfast."

"You're telling me," agreed Sara. "That's how I ended up here. They shipped my job off to Singapore." She finished breakfast and set the bag down. "You boys did good. Ben, let me see that hole in your pants."

Ben put his foot up on the curb so his knee was closer to her eyes. "It's been drafty all morning 'til I stuffed this in there." He pulled out the folded up newspaper from the hole and handed it to Joel.

Sara pulled out a pair of dressmaker's shears engraved with the name *Betsy* and clipped away the loose threads to make the hole smooth. "We'll need to make a patch," she said. "Pull out your shirt but don't get nasty."

Ben pulled out his shirt so the flaps were hanging down. Sara snipped a piece off in the back, placed it over the hole, and pulled out a sewing needle and spool of thread. She sewed it to Ben's pants without once sticking him with the needle. "Me and Betsy can still do a good job. Not bad for an old woman like me."

"Thank you. Thank you," said Ben in astonishment.

"Look at this here." Joel had unfolded the newspaper. "There's going to be a Santa Claus rally tomorrow at City Hall. Maybe we could find Ralph and get him to go. You know, to pass on the favor that woman and her husband talked about."

"We ain't got to do nothin' for them," said Ben. "They gave us money to leave them alone."

"She got us breakfast, and I promised to pass on their favor. Will you help me look for Ralph?"

"Yeah, if you want to."

They spent the rest of the day looking for Ralph who had a large stomach, long white hair that curled around his ears, a ruddy complexion, and the jovial personality of someone who habitually took a couple swigs of wine every now and then. Joel knew he would make a superb Santa. They looked for him down on the Block where the barkers sat on stools outside of striptease clubs and yelled *Come on in and see the ladies dance* and where adult bookstores lined the street, in Canton where Ben played his trumpet and got a whole bunch of folks to contribute coins, and in Fells Point where jazz combos and folk duos played in the pubs. But wherever they went they couldn't find him.

Meanwhile, Peter was putting the finishing touches on his Santa Claus rally. He obtained a city permit for the demonstration, invited the mayor and Bonnie Cartwright, CEO of Grandview Academy, signed a contract with a company to set up a stage and folding chairs, got his church to loan their manger and the rabbi a Star of David and menorah for display, persuaded a Caribbean restaurant to loan a palm tree, and paid an art student at a nearby college to create a cutout of a camel. Then he took his brother to a costume shop and outfitted him in a Santa Claus costume so regal and a fake beard so real it cost $200 a day to rent. He only hoped that everything went as planned and no crazy people crashed their celebration.

The next morning Joel was woken up by a shrieking sparrow being chased 'round and 'round a cedar by a covey of birds that poked and pecked at its prize. In its beak it held a bright orange candy wrapper that was draped over the rest of its body as a cape. Joel's feet were still sore from looking for Ralph all day yesterday so he was rubbing his left sole.

"Are you all right, Joel?" Father Andrew was strolling on the porch of the Roman Catholic Basilica. "I can have someone look at that."

"Naw, that's okay, Father. My pride hurts more than my dogs."

"Do you want to tell me about it?"

"We've been looking for Ralph, but can't find him. We were hoping he could go to the City Hall rally for us dressed up as Santa Claus. You know, to show children that we care."

"That's a noble act, Joel, but sometimes we can't do what we want to. Just remember that God is everywhere and knows our thoughts. If we keep them pure, His kingdom will one day appear before us."

"I don't know about that. I just want to find Ralph."

"I wish you well today." The priest shuffled over to Ben, who was rolling up his sleeping bag, and asked, "How are you doing today?'

"I'm just a bit stiff," admitted Ben, "but it's better sleepin' out here than bein' cooped up in a FEMA trailer. I'll go back to the Ninth Ward when it dries out."

"Everyone in our country is helping your city," stated Father Andrew. "I hope you can go back soon."

"Me too."

The priest stepped back into the cathedral looking solemn.

Now the sparrows were chirping a full-blown chorus as they took turns burrowing into the garden's soil. Joel looked at them for a moment and wondered if God could be sending him a message in a creature so small and insignificant. "Ben," he called, "come here. You got to see this."

"What do you want?"

"Look at them. They're sending me a message."

"Those dumb sparrows?"

"Yeah, man, when I got up they were playing with a candy wrapper and now they're taking a dirt bath. It could be a sign." He gawked at them.

"You're looney like those birds."

"I'm not looney, man," yelped Joel. "They are giving me a message from God."

"I'm gettin' my stuff. Then I'm out of here."

"Why don't you go to the Santa rally with me?"

"How are we goin' to go if we can't find Ralph?"

"I got a way we all can go."

They trotted toward the tent city by the Montgomery Ward's. When they got to the Turk's, they slipped inside. "Hey, Ottah," asked Joel, "can you give us a few cherry pastries?"

"My dear sirs, that is rahat lokum scented with rosewater. By the look of your clothes you must be travelers. Do you have money to pay for my precious goods?"

"Ottah, we'll pay you when we get jobs," insisted Joel. "Right now we're a bit down on our luck."

"I am the third child in my family. That is what my name means. I have four other brothers and sisters. I cannot give you these sweets without receiving payment. I must send a portion of what I make back home. Don't misunderstand me. I am not a cruel Turk. By the grace of Allah I will give you this 50 pound bag of flour." He grunted as he lifted it up and plopped it down. He peered down his nose at the poor fools who had never baked anything before.

"Thanks, Ottah, that's just what we need." Joel slid it off the counter and Ben grabbed the other end. They carried it out of the store.

Ottah was shocked. He looked upward, wrung his hands, and pleaded, "Allah, what have I done to offend you?"

They lugged it toward the tent city, stopping once at the end of the street to get a better grip and another time in Carroll Park to rest on a bench. Joel shook his feet and laced up his boots again while Ben rubbed his sore back. They hiked until they were in the shadow of the abandoned Montgomery Ward building, huffing the whole way.

"Hey, what you got there?" hollered a homeless guy.

"Give me a roll of quarters," quipped another, thinking it was a bank bag.

When they set it on the sidewalk by the parking lot, a few more men came over. "My friends," announced Joel, "will you join us today at the Santa rally."

"The what?"

"The Santa rally. There's going to be a Santa Claus rally at city hall at noon. I'm sure there will be plenty of food and drink there."

"Why should we go?"

"Think of the children."

"Why should we think of them?"

"You were young once. So was I," said Joel. "I remember staying up late on Christmas Eve waiting for Santa's sleigh to slide onto our roof. I would always fall asleep and wake up surprised... 'cause a couple gifts would be sitting underneath our tree."

"I liked the song *I saw Mommy Kissing Santa Claus,"* said another fellow. "If I can smooch a hot mama, I'll dress up." He swirled around in his tattered clothes as though he was dancing.

Other homeless men and women gathered around, thinking that some food was being passed out. They all had ashen faces and stringy hair which was emblematic of sleeping on the streets.

"I liked that song *Chestnuts Roasting on an Open Fire,"* said a third man. "And the smell of food cooking in the kitchen: turkey and dressing, baked potatoes and yams, sweet corn and peas, homemade biscuits and pie."

"That's not what the song was called," retorted an old woman. "It was called *The Christmas Song.* My grandmother bought the original album by Mel Torme. I could listen to that song all day long."

"What about *White Christmas*," someone else said. "My cousin always looked for snowflakes and if it began to snow, all of us would dash to the window and sing that song."

"The food my mother and aunt made during the eight days of Hannukah beat all your Christmas food," said Sara. "We would make matzo ball soup, potato pancakes covered with apple sauce, and Challah, a bread that tastes like French toast."

"Let me say something," said Ben, who pushed himself into the middle of the throng which now numbered over 20 people. "My family celebrated Kwanzaa. That's a Swahili word meanin' *first fruits.* And boy, it would be in the middle of winter and we'd be eatin' fresh watermelon and grapes and peaches and every other fruit you could imagine. We would have drummin' ceremonies and dance and drink wine from a wood chalice carved with wild African animals. Each day of the week we celebrated one of the principles: unity, self-determination, responsibility, cooperation, purpose, creativity, faith. Yeah, I remember. I tell you what… I'll help these kids bring back their holiday."

They continued swapping stories for another half hour. They may have been dressed in rags, but their memories were glorious enough for kings and queens.

"Ben, come over here," said Sara. "Let's see what me and Betsy can do." She pulled out her dressmaker's shears and shaped a piece of curtain by cutting out holes for his head and arms. While she stitched the fabric together to make a red tunic, she remarked, "These fingers are still nimble." Ben tried on her creation and stuffed the stomach with his sleeping bag. Sara tied a rope around his waist and presto!…Santa Claus was standing there.

When the other men saw his change in appearance, nothing could stop them shouting: "Hey, I'm Santa." "No, I'm going to be Santa."

"Everybody who wants to look like Santa please line up," said Joel.

The men staggered into a line.

Joel had cut the bag of flour open with a penknife and dumped some into a metal coffee pot. He added water, lit a fire fueled by cardboard, and brought it to a boil. When he dumped it on a piece of newspaper to cool, it became as thick as syrup. He motioned for the first man to step up. "Chin out."

The fellow leaned forward.

Joel rubbed the homemade glue on the man's chin and hairline. Then he plucked the white stuffing from his sleeping bag and pasted it on, transforming black stubble into a full-fledged snowy-white beard. When the fellow stood straight and slung a cap on his head… presto!…another Santa was made.

Each fellow was smothered with paste and received a white beard and tufts of white hair. Then they were fitted with red tunics cut from either an old curtain, strip of plastic, or other material used to make the tents. In a few minutes, Sara could fashion a garment and two other women stitched it together. Sara's stern expression was replaced by one of joy as she snipped and the other women sewed, cranking out the costumes as though they were working on an assembly line.

They heard the clopping of hooves and looked up. A mounted policeman was riding toward them on a brown horse with a white patch above its nose. "Let's break this up. It's against the law to camp here."

The men rose to their feet and turned toward him.

"What's this?" asked the surprised policeman. "You all look like Saint Nick."

"We're Santa Clauses," said Joel. "We're going to the city hall rally."

"That's what I said. In my country we call him Saint Nick. I was born in Russia, but migrated here after democratic reforms took place. Come on and pack up your things. White Star and I will escort you."

The homeless people stacked their tents and bedrolls in a doorway of the Montgomery Ward building, and the two women volunteered to stay behind to keep watch. The rest of them fell into a jagged line. The policeman led the 25 saints and the Jewish seamstress down Baltimore Street. A patrol car, with its blue-and-red lights flashing, swung into line behind them. People on the sidewalk stopped and gawked. One lady dashed into the street while unbuttoning her coat and said, "Ms. Claus, please take this."

"I can't, Miss," said Sara.

"You can," insisted the woman.

They traded their garments: a worn overcoat with patches on both elbows for a wool hip-length coat with a beautiful red luster and brass buttons. When Sara slipped it on, a long sigh escaped her lips. It was the first time she had felt warm and toasty in several winters.

The regal procession trekked through traffic lights without stopping and turned heads everywhere. Some people gasped. Others snickered. A few grinned and remembered a fond Christmas from their own childhood.

That morning a team of construction workers set up a stage and folding chairs across from city hall. When they arranged the manger, Star of David, menorah, palm tree, and camel cutout on the stage, it resembled an oasis in the Sinai Desert. Food vendors came and set up stands around the plaza: Starbucks served caffe latte and espresso, a farmer's stand offered apple cider, Gino's Grill fried up Italian sausage, Charm City Pizzeria doled out slices, and a hot dog man unfolded a beach umbrella overtop his cart and buttoned a Hawaiian shirt over his sweater to join them. The Turk showed up around 11 a.m., but most of his baked goods remained unsold because he was charging double and triple the regular price. If a potential customer asked him why the cookies and cake slices were so expensive, he would reply, "My dear sir, expensive? I wake up at 4 a.m. and spend two hours preparing my treats from secret family recipes and another three hours baking them and another two hours wrapping them and bringing them here. Do you realize how much gasoline costs these days? I am not a cruel Turk. By the grace of Allah I will allow you to take a whiff." Then he would hold the delicacy under the person's nose and force them to agonize on whether to buy or not. But the truth was he took a nap while the cakes were baking and transported his fare to the rally with a pushcart so the only expense incurred was the wear and tear on his shoes.

The three wise men came early and gave treats to the children: the minister handed out candy canes, the rabbi chocolates in the shape of coins and blue lollipops, and the Imam caramel candies.

Peter stormed the stage and shouted, "It's time to show this city that we still care about Christmas and other religious holidays." The audience whooped and hollered with delight. "Before we have a surprise visit from…" and he whispered…"*Santa Claus*…the Clifton Park Children's Choir will sing several old-fashioned carols."

As the children sang *The Twelve Days of Christmas*, more families showed up to fill the seats. Their rendition of *Silver Bells* included overlapping harmonies. And *Frosty the Snow Man* was so rollicking, everyone sang along. But when they got to *We Wish You A Merry Christmas*, they repeated the chorus so many times that people in the audience began to stir, realizing that something was wrong.

Peter's brother called. Peter tried to act calm, but the three wise men overheard what he said on his cell phone: "You can't back out. Take a taxi!…What do you mean you left your wallet at home?…Hitchhike!…Yes, in a Santa suit!" He hung his head in shame.

The wise men gathered around him.

"What's the matter?" inquired the minister.

"My brother, Roger, might not be able to make it. His van has a flat tire. I don't know what to do."

The three wise men went off in separate directions. The minister crossed his heart and prayed, "Jesus, please show us a miracle." The rabbi chanted a prayer in Hebrew, rocking back and forth in a trance. And the Imam kneeled on a carpet and prayed in Arabic.

A few children in the choir stopped singing and looked around. They begged in a baffled way, "Where's Santa?" "When is Santa coming?"

The choir leader swung his arms wider and sung louder to encourage the others, but more stopped singing.

"My throat is sore," rasped a boy.

"He told us we only had to sing two or three songs," said a girl.

Several parents hurried forward and sang with them, but their prattle continued: "Stop pinching me." "We're supposed to be singing." "Tommy is pulling my hair."

Barb Cartwright strutted onto the stage and roared into the microphone, "This charade has gone on long enough. The School Board is right. There is no Santa Claus."

Peter grabbed the microphone. They wrestled for possession more brutally than bulldogs going after a bone, bruising each other with each elbow thrust. The mayor and his entourage, who were seated in the first row, were perplexed by what was going on. Barb Cartwright shoved Peter aside and moved forward.

He spotted Cynthia, his wife, and Jennifer, his daughter, seated nearby. Both of them had tears welling up in their eyes, looking at a failed husband and father. All his efforts had gone for naught.

"The School Board is authorizing all teachers to give extra homework on December 24th," shrieked Barb Cartwright. "That will keep our students occupied during their long break from school."

The band's playing became as sluggish as a funeral dirge and children in the audience wept in their mothers' arms. Even the three wise men had slumped shoulders and sunken faces.

Then a trumpet blasted the tune *When the Saints Come Marching In* behind them. Everyone turned around and saw Santas marching toward the plaza. Ben was striding in the lead singing, "*Oh, when the Santas…*

And the crowd repeated…

Oh, when the Santas go marching in
All the children will be sleeping

when the Santas go marching in

He played his trumpet again as all the homeless men sang…

We are riding in a sleigh
like we have done before,
and we'll be giving gifts to the young
that they will adore.

Oh, when the Santas, he warbled.
Oh, when the Santas, the crowd sang, *go marching in*
All the children will be sleeping
when the Santas go marching in

"What's this?" screeched Barb Cartwright. "A bunch of old men dressed up in silly costumes."

A construction worker with a *Fear the Fat* T-shirt draped over his beer-belly came over and said, "Sing along or say so long," and bumped her off the stage.

Everyone in the crowd joined in the crescendo of voices, drowning out Barb Cartwright's shrill bickering. The band picked up the tune.

And when the stars, bellowed Ben.

And when the stars, sang the crowd, *light up the sky*
You can count me in that number
when the stars light up the sky

And when Rudolph, bellowed Ben.
And when Rudolph, sang the crowd, *sounds his call*
You can count me in that number
when Rudolph sounds his call

Some say this world of trouble
is the only one we need,
but I'm waiting for Christmas morning
when a new world is revealed to me.

Santas climbed onto the stage. The mayor nodded to his chief of staff. A general reverie prevailed with children smiling and enjoying their candy, parents singing Christmas songs, and people swirling around like the fairies and elves that should have been hanging on the pine tree in the 3rd grade classroom. Several homeless men gathered at the Turk's stand and pawed at his cookies and cakes.

"Don't touch!" barked the Turk, slapping their hands with a serving knife. "My treats are for paying customers. I do not see any coins or dollar bills before me."

"Come on, we're hungry." "Yeah, we ain't eaten all day."

The Imam strolled forward and asked, "What is ailing you, Ottah?"

"The men here are trying to steal my goods. And these are all delicacies."

"We must think of Eid al-Adha and our sacrifice for the poor," said the Imam. "What better way to show Allah's mercy than by sharing?"

"Yes, I understand." To the crowd before him Ottah confessed, "I am not a cruel Turk. By the grace of Allah I will let you gentlemen taste my treats."

They gobbled them up greedily and slurped the goo off their hands and smacked their lips with delight. Ottah looked toward the sky and asked, "Allah, what have I done?"

The next day photos of the Santa Clauses and crowd filled the front page of the newspaper. It proved to all children from pee-wees to teenagers and to all adults with a child still living inside their hearts that there is a Santa Claus and a little good left in the world - from the lowliest street bum to the residents of a gated community. And if someone is lucky on Christmas Eve, they can still see a pack of reindeer and a sleigh streaking across the starry sky.

Inside The Glamorous Life of Lady Plum

"Ryan, don't throw that away!"

It was too late. Her son had already tossed the paper plate into the garbage can.

"Go upstairs and get ready for school!"

"Aw, mom."

"You got to go."

He stood erect and straightened his shoulders, "Mom, when are you getting me a firehouse dog? My friend, Tommy, says we can buy one at PetSmart."

"They're called Dalmatians," she corrected him. "You have to do your homework every day and maybe we'll see."

"I don't feel like waiting until my birthday," he whined. "I want one now."

"You can't have one now. You know what your father said."

"Aw, mom."

Her son was still whining as he climbed the stairs. How many times did they have to go through this? She scooted over to the can and found the plate. The cream cheese and bagel was only half-eaten. She slid one end into her mouth. Didn't her children realize how expensive food was? Cheese was $4.59 a pound. Her son had thrown it into the trash as though it meant nothing. The whole family had to help make ends meet.

"Waaah!"

"What's wrong with you?" She spun around and looked over her daughter's pajamas. There were no spills or leaks anywhere. "Hon', can you come down and get Jenny?"

Her husband tramped downstairs, buttoning his shirt, "I'm already late for work."

"Can you get her dressed?"

"Why is it always me? Why can't you get her dressed?"

"Because I'm cleaning up their mess."

Her husband grabbed the kid and swung her around. "Up we go. Come on."

Jenny giggled with delight as her dad carried her upstairs.

"Where'd you put your orange juice?" She looked underneath the table, but the cup wasn't there. She rooted around in the trash can again. There it was. A few gulps were left in the bottom. $2.99 a carton. She couldn't remember the last time she had eaten a normal breakfast. She was always finishing what her children left behind. Her married life had made her a scavenger.

"Ev…elynnnnn, where's my blue suit?" her husband's voice carried from upstairs.

How did she know? She sucked in a big breath and yodeled, "It's where you left it."

She heard the stomping of his feet overhead. "Did you pick it up at the cleaners?"

"Hon', you got the ticket," she yelled back.

She heard him slam the closet door upstairs. "Ev…elynnnn, why can't you help around here? Is that too much to ask?"

She couldn't stand the way her husband pronounced her name when he was angry. He always emphasized the V as though it was a dagger and slurred the ending. She wished her mother had given her a name that had a sweet sound when it flowed out of a person's mouth. A name like Susan or Melanie. When she was a girl, everyone called her Sinead. Then her parents got divorced and her dad and stepmother decided she should use her middle name: Evelyn. Her girlfriend down the street called her Teri because that's what she looked like - a smaller version of Teri Hatcher with shoulder-length brunette hair and dark, suggestive eyes. And her last name, forget it. She took her husband's name, Johnson, when she married him. It ended up being misspelled on the deed to the house and now she received mail addressed to a woman known as Ms. Johanson from credit card companies, car insurers, and bulk mail advertisers. She couldn't get a break anywhere.

She hustled upstairs and slipped on a navy blouse and tan skirt. Her clothes did not match anymore. That was another condition of being married. She peered into the mirror and covered a bruise on her cheek with some makeup and hid the dark bags under her eyes. Had she slept on the side of her face last night? Jenny was howling again. Her husband had already walked out the front door. The rest of her makeup would have to wait. She grabbed her pocketbook and galloped downstairs. Jenny was still wailing as she led her by the hand. "Ryan, lock the door." She buckled Jenny into the safety seat. Ryan was lugging his books. He got in. The tires screeched as the SUV bolted out of the driveway. She zoomed down the road. Jenny stopped howling and wore a look of wonderment on her face. Why did the SUV always lull her into a tranquil state like a baby carriage? They needed to make one small enough to drive around inside the house.

She pulled down the window visor and fished in her pocketbook for her compact. It was back home on the dresser. She couldn't put on that touch of rouge that made her face look human. Now she would have to spend the day looking like the ghost she had become. She pressed her lips together and smeared them with lipstick, then wiped away the excess with a tissue. The other cars honked as she wove through traffic, which was heavier than normal since it was Christmas Eve. She let the SUV idle as she dropped Jenny off at the daycare center. Then she lead-footed the quarter mile to Ryan's school and roared to a stop in front of the long sidewalk leading up to the main door. "Let's not have any trouble today." Her son jumped out, but forgot to shut the door. She leaned over and pulled it closed. A NASCAR driver could not drive any faster to the Metro station. She wove in and out of traffic, tailgated other cars, and slung by in their draft. She did everything but bump them off the road. She raced into the lot, parked, and hurried down the steps into the station.

She swiped her pass card over the screen, but banged into the turnstile. It would not budge.

"Miss, I need to see your monthly pass and some identification," came an ominous voice from the booth.

She pranced over and gave the attendant her pass card. His frail frame did not match the booming voice. She opened her pocketbook and got out her gym membership card.

"I need to see a driver's license."

Her license had a dreadful photo taken under the glare of fluorescent lights.

"This can't be right, Miss. Do you have another form of identification?"

"I'm not applying for a mortgage, you know." She slipped her grocery store cash card in front of him.

The attendant had a baffled look on his face. "On your driver's license it says you're 38, but your gym membership card says 33."

"I subtracted five years from my birth date. I thought if I exercised every day it would make me look younger."

"And this card," the attendant was holding up the grocery store cash card, "it says you're only 28."

"I was with friends when I applied for that, you know."

"No, I don't know. You look like you're in your 40s or 50s."

"Forties or 50s?" she groaned. "I might feel that old. I have two kids running me ragged, but I'm certainly not 40 or 50."

The man looked at her again. "There's a lot of gray in your hair."

"Oh, my God, I'll go to the hairdresser at lunch. Is that okay? Please let me through?"

Another attendant moseyed over. "What's going on?"

"All the ages are screwed up on her identification forms."

The other attendant gathered up the cards and handed them to her. "We understand, ma'am, typo errors. They don't teach math in school like they used to."

A train had pulled into the station. The last riders were getting aboard. Their number was shrinking on the platform as she dashed toward a car. The bells sounded. All the doors were closing. She dove through a crease and stumbled inside. Most of the seats were filled. She hustled past a man standing in the aisle. An elderly woman was heading toward the same empty seat she was. She slipped around her and plopped down. The woman gasped, "Huh!", but continued down

the aisle. There was a puff of air as the brakes were released, and then the train rolled down the tracks.

She was sleepy. She always had to choose between sleep or food. Either her kids kept her up all the time, which made her sleepy, or she had to chase after them and run an endless list of errands for her husband, which made her hungry. This morning she had stuffed some food in her mouth. But sleep? The subway car gently rocked from side to side. A stray wheel was going clackity-clack against the rail. The air was stuffy and hot inside…

Lady Plum could hear the patter of horse hooves on the paved roadway. The carriage rocked back and forth and came to a stop. Lord Oliver swung the door open. She strutted toward a stone building that looked like a medieval castle. A light was shining from behind her onto the entrance. Then she saw the sun directly in front of her. She slowly spun around. The coach she had ridden in glittered because it was made of solid gold. The frame, the doors, the bolts that held it together. Everything. Lady Plum followed her guardian. A servant opened the door to a banquet hall and a trumpet sounded. The doorman called out, "Lord Oliver and Our Lady Plum." Lord Oliver was a rotund gentleman who moved with an aura of refinement. Lady Plum had an exquisite figure that was the envy of every woman standing before her. Their mouths were agape. Men bowed low before her, but they couldn't take their eyes off her. Lord Oliver and Lady Plum were seated at an enormous banquet table. A side door opened and a line of servants paraded forth carrying trays of food raised over their heads. They all had the arms of bodybuilders because the trays were stacked with food of such quantity and weight that the word, huge, was too small for any single dish. One tray held a roasted pig weighing 250 pounds with a garnish of 75 baked apples. Another tray contained…

A man staggered toward her and slurred, "Hey, baby doll, got some spare change?"

She drew back her hands and hissed, "Get away!"

The man plodded down the aisle of the subway car, bumping into people.

She wondered if all the men in her life were drunks. Sometimes she could smell alcohol on her boss's breath when he came back from lunch. And her husband would come home drunk after spending the evening with his brother at a Nationals baseball game. He would wake her up at one in the morning and threaten her. Was she blocking out the physical abuse she received from him? She was tired of covering up the bruises on her face with makeup. Maybe that was where they were coming from. And what about her son, Ryan? He always seemed to be so withdrawn from the world. Was he also being physically abused? She clutched her pocketbook against her chest and rocked back and forth. She had to fall asleep again to find Lady Plum. She had to keep on holding on…

The odor was as sweet as honey. What was it? Yes, mint jelly. A servant was carrying a tray containing two pheasants as stout as turkeys. One was stuffed with oyster dressing and the other with mint jelly. A third tray held venison with two racks of ribs sticking straight up into the air. There were baskets of limes and lemons and oranges. That was followed by a swordfish six feet long with its sword and tail fins hanging over opposite ends of the tray. A buttery smell came from the sauce it was basted in. The servants brought forth loaves of bread, bowls of mashed potatoes, various succotash and soups, sauerkraut, tossed salads showered with bits of bacon and bread crumbs, and still more in an endless parade of plenty.

A servant scooped wine from the top of a barrel that was 10 feet tall and almost as wide.

He came back and filled their wineglasses to the brim. From her vantage point, Lady Plum could see the rosy color of the wine at the rim while deep below the color had become as dark as storm clouds gathering on the horizon. Another servant turned the knob of an iron spigot at the bottom and a frothy slush flowed out. He filled bottles with Thunderbird and Mad Dog labels. The bottles were given to homeless men with withered faces who wore tattered clothes with holes in the sleeves, patches on the pants, and boots splitting apart at the seams. The men tottered back and forth on their feet and grinned when they received their bottles, showing off the dark gaps in their teeth. Lady Plum felt safe on her pedestal away from their leering eyes and foul breaths.

Lord Oliver spoke, "Gracious guests, I have been informed that a storm is coming in from the coast. It will be here in less than an hour. Therefore, our Lady Plum will only select one person to perform this evening to cap off our holiday celebration."

A man whose muscles rippled in yellow leotards slunk in as stealthily as a cat. "My Lady Plum, I can stand on my hand." He did a handstand with only one hand and continued speaking, "I can whirl across the floor swifter than a dervish and tumble with more energy than a bouncing ball. Please let me entertain you."

A second man dressed in a grand tuxedo - its elegant tail grazing the floor - waltzed in.

"I can thrill you with any card trick." He shaped a deck of cards into a lady's fan and picked out four aces without looking. "I can make animals appear and disappear." He pulled a white dove from his top hat and released it into the air. "I can cut a lady in half and put her back together again. Please select me."

A third man strolled in strumming a guitar. His eyes were as brilliant as sapphires. "My La-la-la-lady Plum, I can sing romantic ballads in either English, French, or Latin. Which would you prefer?"

"My Lady Plum, I believe I was here first," said the acrobat who was now doing pushups with only one finger.

The magician disappeared in a puff of smoke and reappeared on the other side of him. "Pardon me."

The singer was humming a song.

This was too much to bear. All three of these gentlemen were trying to win her heart and she could only choose one. She was on the verge of deciding. The name of the man was on her lips...

Someone was shaking her shoulder. She could see a blue uniform through the slit of her left eye. The train conductor? She must have missed her stop. She would be late to work. Her boss would yell at her and possibly fire her. She had to fix it. She would stop at Dunkin Donuts and get a dozen filled with raspberry jam. Her boss liked those. She could say she had to wait in line for a whole hour. On the way home from work she could stop off at the Humane Society Shelter on Bradley Street and pick up a dog for her son. It wouldn't have to be a pure breed Dalmatian. Any spotted dog would do. That would put a smile on his face. But her husband might get mad. He had to be pacified. Eureka! She would fix his favorite meal: pork chops simmered in homemade gravy. As soon as he opened the front door, the odor alone would melt his heart. She knew she could do these things if only she had time…

Her eyes popped open. A policeman was standing in front of her. He had a stern look on his face and spoke slowly, "Your royal highness, you can't sleep in the park. You have to move on."

Nearby there was some shouting and the metallic ring of trash cans. Rubbish was being dumped into the back of a truck with the grinding noise drowning out the cooing of a flock of pigeons. Wind whipped across an iceberg formed by frozen water in a stone fountain. Well-dressed men and women were scooting through the park swinging their briefcases. They did not glance in her direction.

She stood up and made sure all the buttons on her tattered coat were fastened. She picked up a shopping bag that contained all of her belongings - a pair of thick cotton socks, a crusty bun she found in the trash yesterday evening, a plastic tarp to cover herself in case of a cloudburst, a paper cup with a few quarters in it - and started to walk away. She wished she was old enough to collect social security. Then she could rent a room of her own. She could fall asleep for as long as she wanted and bake cinnamon buns for breakfast. And nobody would dare wake her up in the morning. One day the government would be sending her checks in the mail if only she could remember her name and age.

Rebounders

A purple haze colored the evening sky, marking a northeaster bearing down on their sleepy Maryland town, and causing the East Side High gymnasts to look out the field house window and watch ice pellets bouncing off the ground.

"I told you, Tasha," declared Sophie. "In my country a hailstorm is an omen that something bad will happen."

"Maybe werewolves will attack us," teased Robin, a slim African-American girl who was a senior. She pranced off to practice her floor routine.

It reminded Natasha of a place always cold and dreary where it rained or snowed every other day. "We're in America now," she replied. "We must forget where we're from."

"In Romania it means something bad will happen," said Sophie. "The same is true here."

Natasha and Sophie, who had flat faces and dark hair, still spoke with slight eastern European accents and formed a clique on the team. They stood there for a while, then a whistle blew and a high-pitched voice called out, "Get her down from there, Chad!"

Prudence, a girl with a blonde ponytail from Bridgeport, Connecticut was perched in-between the still rings in an Iron Cross position with her arms straight out and her head just above their plane. She let go and flopped into Chad's arms. Then she hustled off the mat.

"I'm helping her to strengthen her shoulders," said Chad. "We have to get them ready for the town championship. The earlier we start the better."

"I determine what exercises the girls perform," scolded Coach Jayne, who was in her twenties and had a boyish haircut. The lines on her face deepened. "We can't have two head coaches on this team. Do you understand that, Chad?"

"Yes, Coach Jayne." Chad's body slumped. Even though he was a husky fellow who once made it to the nationals, he was subordinate to their coach.

Coach Jayne blew the whistle again. "Let's move on to the vault!"

The team lined up behind one another at the 80-foot long mat that led to the apparatus. Robin and Prudence stood in the front. Sophie and Natasha followed, and the rest of the girls made up the rear.

Coach Jayne furrowed her brow and snapped out commands, "Sophie get behind Robin. Natasha follow Prudence. Make sure you spot each other. Watch out for your teammates."

"Yes, Coach Jayne," replied the girls in unison.

Chad had taken a position behind the horse where he could be the first spotter. Robin ran down the runway…

Meanwhile, Natasha winced. She despised following Prudence in the practice rotation. Last year that girl only said one word to her. Natasha had slipped off the balance beam and fell to the floor. While she gathered herself to stand up, Prudence came over and quipped, "Amateur." Then the shrew strutted off.

Prudence dashed toward the apparatus quicker than a racehorse sprinting down the stretch at the Preakness. She hit the springboard with a whop, pushed off the table with her hands, did one and a half twists in midair, and stuck the landing.

"Good form," called out Coach Jayne. "Definitely a 9.7 or .8."

Natasha was next. She rubbed her hands in the chalk to get a firm push. When she jogged down the runway, she kept increasing her speed. She hit the springboard and was thrown forward. She stuck out her hands and pushed off the table. One hand slipped, but she was propelled through the air. She did a giant somersault without bending her arms or legs and landed on the mat, taking a step back to keep from falling.

"Sprint down that mat and strike the springboard," called out Coach Jayne. "You need to hustle to complete the forward layout."

It was always the same following Prudence. Even as sophomores Natasha was no match to that girl. The year before she sat on the bench while Prudence competed at every meet. It irked her.

Coach Jayne blew the whistle and barked, "Chad, take these girls to the uneven bars."

"Yes, coach," he replied.

They strode over to the uneven bars while Coach Jayne stayed behind with the newcomers to work on their vaults. The rookies - Lynn, Serena, and Charlotte - were country girls who knew about southern fried chicken, social etiquette, crab cakes, and NASCAR. They formed their own clique. They had to learn the basics the way Natasha did last year.

Robin performed her routine on the uneven bars. Even though this was only their second practice of the season, her movements were fluid. Sophie was next. She worked on the lower bar, wheeling round and round. She released toward the higher bar, but lost her grip and flopped to the mat. "Chalk up better," stated Chad.

Prudence was next. She leaped onto the lower bar, wheeled round and round, and transitioned to the higher bar with a flawless release. As she spun around and around, Robin yelled, "Way to go, Prue."

Prudence had a thin, angular face and lanky body reflective of her Nordic heritage. Her family, which had roots in New England, moved to Maryland to take advantage of the gymnastics program. Even so she remained aloof and only befriended Robin, who maintained the same skill set. They formed the team's third clique.

Prudence gathered more speed and twirled round. She dismounted by doing a somersault with a full twist and landed solid, only taking a tiny hop at the end.

Natasha made sure to rub plenty of chalk on her hands. She took a deep breath. She stepped up to the lower bar and swung underneath. When she pulled herself on top in a prone position, her ribs ached, telling her to strengthen her abs. She stood atop the lower bar and released toward the higher one. Grabbing onto the bar, she wheeled around in a slow loop. The tension on her arms would turn into throbbing if she just hung onto the upper bar so she leaped to the lower bar and worked herself up to the higher one again. She was preparing for the dismount when she lost her grip, hanging on with one hand.

The centrifugal force of the circular movement jerked her off. She cartwheeled off the mat and landed on the hardwood floor with a thud. Her leg seared as though stuck with a thousand needles. She howled in anguish.

"I'm sorry, Tasha," said Sophie, cringing. "I should have caught you. I knew something bad would happen. The hailstorm warned us."

Prudence trotted over, looked down, and said, "You're done for the season." Then she strolled away as Coach Jayne and the other teammates rushed toward her.

The girls had shocked looks, half of them feeling sorry for her and the rest being scared that an ill-timed move might make them fall and injure themselves.

Chad stooped down and cradled her in his arms. His biceps bulged as he carried her out of the fieldhouse.

A jeep pulled up. Coach Jayne called out, "Put her on the backseat."

Chad nestled her into the jeep, which screeched out of the parking lot. Every time the tires hit a bump her foot ached.

"Every gymnast gets injuries," explained Coach Jayne. "You can expect a dozen during your career. A foot injury is not a major one even if it is broken."

"Do you think it's broken?" asked Natasha.

"I don't know," replied the coach. "When I was a couple years older than you, I hurt my spine doing a vault. A MRI showed that I cracked a vertebra. It ended my career, but I can still coach and be a part of the sport."

"I don't want to be a coach," murmured Natasha.

Coach Jayne smirked and said, "It's not that bad."

In the hospital emergency room, Dr. O'Keefe, the physician on duty, prodded and poked Natasha's foot, causing her to squeal and squirm.

"Humph." He peered down at her through his bifocals and stated, "You have torn ligaments above the ankle." He put her foot in a protective cast and prescribed pain killers.

Natasha cried when her mother arrived to pick her up. They stopped at a grocery store to get the medication and two quarts of cookie dough ice cream. When Natasha arrived home, she plopped on the sofa in the living room and turned on the TV to a channel she hadn't watched since she was a child. She spooned the ice cream treat and tried to chuckle at the antics of the cartoon characters though she felt glum.

Her father came home later that evening. He was a short, balding man who often worked late. While the other girls' parents were still youthful or suffering midlife crisis, her parents were mature, less than a decade away from collecting social security. Her father kneeled by the sofa to inspect her cast and said, "I hope it doesn't hurt too much. How serious is it?"

"Do you have to ask?" whined Natasha. "Prudence said I'm done for the season."

"She tore several ligaments above her ankle," disclosed her mother. "Dr. O'Keefe said it's similar to a hamstring pull. After a period of prolonged rest, it should heal itself."

"As long as you're all right," said her father, stroking her chin.

***

Her parents went into the kitchen to drink their tea. Neither one of them said a word. That was the foot that allowed them to adopt their daughter. When they first saw her in person at the orphanage, she held a music box adorned with a miniature photo of the Bolshoi Ballet. Whenever she lifted the lid, a tiny ballerina popped up and twirled around to a classical tune. They thought that was the cause of her affliction. Even though the music box was stolen by a caretaker at the orphanage and pawned for 1,200 rubles on the black market the day before they boarded the jet, when they arrived home in America their tiny daughter often swirled around like a whirlwind and fell on the floor.

They had her club foot repaired by a surgeon at Johns Hopkins. In her birth nation of Russia this was not allowed because a health panel, which based its decisions on 80 years of socialized medicine, would not grant approval. Only children born to families connected with the Kremlin or who could afford to pay a bribe received official authorization. But the cause of her obsession with gymnastics ran deeper than that. Only their daughter knew where it came from.

***

Natasha watched one cartoon after another, sometimes remembering an episode from years earlier. She felt comfortable on the sofa with a pair of large pillows for support.

"Natasha, come to dinner," said her mother.

She pouted and whined, "I'm not hungry."

"Your father has fixed you a rib-eye steak just the way you like it - seared on both sides and cooked to a medium-rare."

"I want more ice cream," she demanded.

"I'll get you a quart of cookie-dough."

"Mother, you know I eat Raspberry Ripple in the evening."

"Raspberry Ripple?"

"It's vanilla ice cream with raspberry syrup swirled in-between."

"I know what it is...Okay."

***

Natasha's mom poked her head into the kitchen and said, "I'll go to the store to get her ice cream."

"I'll keep dinner warm until you get back," replied her husband.

Her mother put on her coat and went out to start the car. The wind howled overtop a snow drift a foot high. She recalled a place twelve years ago where the snow drifts were five times as tall and the wind rumbled down from the North Pole sounding like it was talking to you. It could make a person go insane. As the cab driver drove them to the orphanage, there were motorists stranded on the side of the road with broken down Yugoslavian cars and buses. Nothing ran on time in a society where a premium was placed on perfection because there was no incentive to do anything right. The stranded motorists stared back at them with looks of desperation, and the cab driver dare not stop for fear of being robbed.

They thought about going back to the airport without even stopping at the orphanage, but her husband said, "We must have faith. Maybe this time will be different."

It was. After they brought Natasha home, the joy came back into their lives. Her mother was sure that her daughter would one day practice ballet and become a prima ballerina for a dance company. Instead, Natasha chose gymnastics. She never understood why. Now this. Her mother worried that Natasha might have a more serious injury, possibly crippling, in the future. Even so she decided to keep pouring her love into her daughter. She hurried to the grocery store and brought the ice cream. She came back with two quarts of Raspberry Ripple. Her daughter spooned the sweet treat lounging in the living room while they ate in the kitchen.

***

For the next two weeks Natasha remained propped up on the plush sofa. She ate, slept, watched TV, made phone calls, and did her homework there. At school she used a crutch to get back and forth between classrooms. Even so, her body was overloaded with carbohydrates, making her feel sluggish. And her mental time clock went awry, waking her in the middle of the night and causing her parents to express concern.

On a Saturday morning her mother came into the living room and announced, "Your father and I would like to give you your Christmas presents."

"It's not even Thanksgiving," replied Natasha, trying to arrange the facts in her mind. "Only children with cancer get presents early." A horrible thought came to her. "Do I have gangrene?"

"Gangrene?"

"They're cutting off my foot, aren't they?"

"No, honey," replied her mother. "Dr. O'Keefe says you're getting better. We want to celebrate Christmas early. I got you this." Her mother handed her a little gift covered in paper with printed candy canes.

During her first Christmas celebration her parents hung candy canes from every limb of an evergreen. Whenever she tottered by, she grabbed one to suck on. The memory seemed so fresh as she peeled off the wrapping. She lifted a lid off a box and saw shiny custom-made gymnast shoes, which looked like slippers but with firmer support for her heels and toes.

Natasha was puzzled because she had been limping around the house for what seemed like eons. She muttered, "Thanks, mama."

"Your father has another present for you downstairs."

She followed her mother down the steps into the basement, using a crutch to lessen the weight on her injured foot. Her father was setting up a stationary bicycle.

"This will help you get back in shape," he said while tinkering on the wheel.

When her mother turned around, the crutch was leaning against the wall. Muffled footsteps and moaning came from upstairs.

"I got it fixed," stated her father. "Where's Natasha?'

"We've upset her," said her mother. "I think she's in her room crying."

He tightened a screw on the pedal and said, "You can lead a horse to water, but…"

Suddenly, Natasha was standing there in her gym shorts and T-shirt. She hopped forward and hugged him. "Thanks, papa." She mounted the bike and started peddling, the wheel whining as it spun.

"Here's an instruction manual," said her mother.

Natasha focused on the bike, adjusting the controls. The wheel whined louder as she went faster.

Her father put his arm around her mother and confided, "I think our daughter is back."

Natasha pedaled the bike until she was famished. Her mother fixed her a warm bowl of soup. Then she was back at it again. Her parents couldn't keep her away. She worked out at home for an entire week, riding more and more miles on the stationary bike. The following Saturday she was stretching her legs on the sofa when her mother called out, "Natasha, someone is here to see you."

Sophie, still wrapped in her winter coat, stepped into the living room and stood about five feet away. "I wanted to see how you are doing," said her friend. "I'm sorry about what happened. I can go."

"Sophie," said Natasha, hopping toward her, "don't be silly."

The girls hugged.

"The accident was my fault," said Sophie. "I should have caught you."

"I shouldn't try to do a release with one hand."

They broke their hug and stood apart. Sophie tossed her winter coat on a chair. Both of them looked at the coffee table in the living room.

Natasha blurted, "I'm the lobster."

"I'm the crab," replied Sophie.

They moved the coffee table out of the way. Then they both did hand stands with their legs bent at the knees. They turned their backs toward each other and advanced against the other crustacean. Natasha bent her head up to peek at the crab while Sophie twisted her head to one side as far as she could to view the lobster. They spurred with each other, punching with their legs. When they came tumbling down in a tangled mess, both of them giggled.

It was the first time since her injury that Natasha felt happy.

"When are you coming back?" asked Sophie.

"Next week," said Natasha. "Dr. O'Keefe is cutting off my cast, but says I shouldn't land on my feet from any height more than five feet."

"No vault or uneven bars?"

"No. I'll work on my floor routine and the beam."

"That's cool."

The cast was cut off, and Natasha returned to practice. When she entered the field house, with its high ceiling and tinted windows, it resembled a cathedral. Instead of kneeling on an altar, she would perform her routines to show her devotion. And at the beginning of each event she would dip her hands or feet into a bowl of chalk the way the faithful dipped their heads in a river to become baptized. It was with this awe that Natasha worked her way through the floor routine and performed exercises on the balance beam, overcoming the aches and pains in her muscles and joints.

"Coach Jayne," said Chad. "You got the girls sweating this afternoon."

"Chad, girls don't sweat," retorted the coach. "Men sweat. Girls perspire."

"Call it what you will."

The smell of chalk and perspiration was intoxicating to Natasha, who couldn't get enough. For the next few weeks she worked out in the gym whenever a teammate was there. The only girl who logged more time was Prudence. The difference between them was that Prudence attacked each routine as though performing before the judges. Her countenance became grim - her routines replicated. The only time she changed her work pattern was if Coach Jayne snapped commands to make her improve a technique or repeat an element. Meanwhile Natasha would first attempt to get her muscles warmed up and loose. Once that happened she felt as light as a butterfly and as relaxed as someone laying on a beach during summer. Natasha felt as though she could roll, spin, bounce, leap, and tumble all day long. Her mouth would be open slightly to allow her to breathe, making it appear that she was grinning. The other girls did their elements one at a time as though performing calisthenics, griping about the difficulty of the movement or complaining about minor aches and pains.

Coach Jayne called the girls together one afternoon and declared, "It's time to start preparing for the town championship. I will be evaluating each teammate's routine and suggesting improvements. We also have one more meet as a dress rehearsal."

Each girl went off to a different apparatus to practice their routine. Coach Jayne stood by the uneven bars, blowing her whistle and shouting out commands. Chad went over to the vault to spot several girls. Natasha practiced her floor routine. After each move she stopped and twirled to the left or right to take a big step. The whistle blew nearby. Coach Jayne shouted, "Stop admiring yourself after each element. Make your routine fluid."

Natasha placed her hands on her hips, elbows out, and stared at the coach.

"Go back to the beginning," ordered Coach Jayne.

Natasha trotted back to the corner of the mat. Another girl rewound the tape recorder and pressed the *play* button. While she performed each element to the music, Coach Jayne shouted instructions. When the scrutiny was over, Coach Jayne scolded another girl. The practice ended at 5:30 p.m. One by one the girls left the field house. Only Natasha and Prudence remained behind to practice some more. Eventually Prudence left.

It was 6:30 p.m. Coach Jayne walked over to Natasha's mom and said, "Ms. Fuller, here is the key. Lock up and return it to my office tomorrow morning."

"Okay, Jayne."

Natasha saw her coach leave. Even so she kept running across the mat, somersaulting, and springing back up into the air. When she realized that her mother had nodded off on the bench, a sense of glee filled her because she could practice as much as she wanted.

After Natasha was sure that her floor routine flowed with one element following the other without any breaks, she stopped and toweled off. Then she plodded toward the balance beam. She kept being drawn back to the beam even though it was the most difficult apparatus to master. Performing any routine on it was an act of heroics. She recalled holding a music box, which she had received as a gift with her breakfast, on a snowy Christmas morning in Leningrad 12 years earlier. She did not know what it was or why the little figurine popped up and twirled about when she lifted the lid.

The state orphanage was operating on a skeleton staff with most of the nurses and caregivers staying home to be with their families. Some attended mass at an eastern orthodox church; others invited relatives to share a meal in their cramped apartments and to read the Bible. Only two employees, a young woman without a husband and a maintenance worker, dashed from room to room, making sure the children were fed and occupied with an activity, the older ones taking care of the younger ones. These were the children that no one in Russia wanted who had birth defects and were not suitable for a perfect society.

That afternoon the television was left on in her ward. The state controlled station showed reruns of Russian athletes in the winter and summer Olympics - skiers sloshing down slopes, weightlifters grunting under heavy burdens, and others. Natasha recalled the acrobatics of Olga Korbut at a summer Olympics. She was drawn to the apparatus because that was her first memory of something beautiful: an athlete performing a ballet on the beam as grand as a dance in Swan Lake. The pigtailed *sparrow of Minsk* pranced across the beam and performed one backward handspring after another. Then the 17-year old wowed the audience with a back aerial flip, the first one ever performed in international competition. And now after so many exercises to get ready to step onto the beam and so many times falling off, getting bruises all over her body, Natasha was still drawn back.

She mounted the plank and practiced walking across, which seemed so simple to a fan of the sport, but was so difficult to do. First the beam was only four inches wide. Second, it stood four feet high, causing any normal person to hold out their arms to maintain their balance. During practice Coach Jayne would yell, "You know you can walk its length. Use that confidence. Hold your arms at your sides to score points on the artistry."

Natasha practiced doing a forward somersault. Once again it looked simple, but the movement had to be continuous and she had to stay on the narrow plank. She fell off again and again, but remounted the apparatus. Finally, she practiced a back somersault. That was what made Olga Korbut's performance at the Olympics so powerful. Only a few gymnasts could master the move. Unfortunately, Natasha wasn't one of them. She fell off again and again. She kept working on the elements until every muscle in her body ached. Then she went into the locker room to put on her street clothes.

Natasha tugged on her mother's coat to wake her and said, "Mama, I'm ready to go."

It was 10:30 p.m. They shuffled out to the car in the chill of the night. The ride home was quiet because she was exhausted from practicing and her mother was concentrating on the road, trying to remain awake.

The aroma of a cooked meal greeted them at home. Putting dinner on the kitchen table, her father said, "I fixed you chicken breast, green beans sautéed with almonds, and mashed potatoes made with skim milk, no butter."

Natasha plopped on a chair and dug in with a folk. She whined, "What's this?"

"What's what, dear?" asked her mother.

"I don't eat chicken skin," she huffed. "It's greasy and fattening."

"I'm sorry, Natasha," said her father.

She dug in again, devouring huge mouthfuls. Her father gave her a second helping. She ate more than both of them combined. She got up and said, "Thank you, papa." Fifteen minutes later she was curled up in bed sound asleep.

The next morning she strutted through the house and screeched, "Come on. I'm going to be late." It was 6 a.m. Natasha had already eaten breakfast. She screeched again, "When are we going? I want to get an hour in before school starts."

"I'm coming," said her mother, getting her coat out of the closet. "I'm coming."

Her mother went outside and started the car. Natasha heard her scraping ice off its windows. She came out of the house bundled up in a sweat jacket with the hood pulled over her head. Plopping into the shotgun seat, she felt how warm the car's interior was. She wanted to thank her mother, but was anxious about not being at practice yet. The car went fast because the roads were clear. She dashed to the locker room while her mother dropped off the key at the coach's office.

When Natasha shuffled into the field house, she heard huffing coming from across the floor. Prudence was already there. That early bird began her morning workouts at 4 a.m. Neither one of them spoke to each other though they would peek at their teammate practicing. They worked out on different routines until the school bells rung.

December rolled on. Natasha watched Charlotte compete in her place at a meet with a Podunk high school in southern Maryland. East Side High evened their record at 2 wins and 2 losses. The town championship, which was held at the mid-point of the season, was coming up. It was important to the team because the town's two high schools, one on the east side that catered to working class families and the other on the west side for upscale suburban dwellers, competed in everything from academic achievement to sports. Coach Jayne penciled her in for the floor routine. She would wear the blue and white school colors again. She put more effort into her practices, coming in as early and staying as late as she could.

Two days before Christmas the meet took place. When the girls boarded the bus, they bounced up the steps. They passed by the local gas station which had assembled a four-foot Christmas tree made of iron hubcaps, rowhouses with an occasional string of colored lights, the barber shop with a hand written sign reading, *Happy Holidays*, and the toy store which featured a two-foot tall Santa figurine. In the middle of town strings of silver tinsel were strung across the street from one house or business to another. The bus rolled into the more affluent West Side. Neon signs at the department store announced a Christmas sale, the car dealership had an inflatable Santa that stood 20 feet tall, and detached single family homes shined with clusters of colored lights. When they pulled into the parking lot at West Side High, a 10-foot tall sign read, *Home of the Titans*. They filed out of the bus as a solemn group. While they dressed in the visitors' locker room, they wondered if any fans were out there to support their team. A half hour before the meet started, they marched into the field house to warm up. While most of the West Side fans showed up in suits and dresses, some of their fans arrived in jeans and slacks. They heard the chant, "Go Wildcats," from some parts of the crowd.

Their opponents, the Titans, were already by their bench. The Titans were tough, gritty competitors who were giants in the sport ranging in height from 4'8" to 5'4". However, there were several girls on Natasha's team that were actually taller. Prudence came in at a lengthy 5'6" and Robin had spurted to 5'7". Still the Titans were the town's defending champions and had won the coveted trophy three years in a row, causing some girls on the Wildcats to downplay the importance of winning the championship. Lynn quipped, "Who needs that stupid jug?" And Robin, who was already inundated by offers of college scholarships in gymnastics and soccer, simply said, "If there's no money involved, it's not important."

Natasha did some tumbles on the floor mat and returned to the bench. She looked for her parents in the stands. The other members of her team returned from their warm ups. The girls' faces became hardened as the start time neared. Coach Jayne wanted her girls to be as tough as nails and as gritty as a football team so no whimpering, crying, or carrying-on was allowed from their bench.

A frail man with gaunt facial features, snow-white hair, and gnarled fingers prattled to the judges. He stepped up to the microphone and sucked in a deep breath that made his shoulders square. Then he announced in a booming voice that filled up the field house, "Welcome, ladies and gentlemen, to the town championship. Over on my right, from East Side High, we have the Wildcats."

Wearing their white leotards with blue trim, Natasha and the other girls stood up and waved to the crowd, drawing a smattering of applause.

"And over here on my left from West Side High are the defending…" and the man elongated each syllable "champions, the Titans."

Those girls slipped off their sweats to reveal bright red leotards. A blonde-haired boy romped around the field house waving a red flag with the name, Titans, in gold letters. Thunderous applause and cheers erupted.

****

Natasha's mother shuddered. She recalled a time years ago when they adopted their daughter. Red flags flew from every flag pole in Russia even though refugees from the Chernobyl nuclear disaster still flooded the cities and the economy had collapsed, crushing each citizen's dreams. The elderly slept in subway stations or out in a city's parks, too poor to afford housing, and many begged in the streets for rubles so they could buy food which had skyrocketed in price. There was a period of détente between Russia and America as the great bear begged the West to send grain and bailout money. She and her husband travelled to Leningrad and tramped up the steps of every ministry building in Palace Square. They did all they could to save one girl from a life of ridicule and suffering, filling out countless forms and emptying their wallets to grease the palms of public officials, each one acting like a bigger buffoon than the one before.

They thought about giving up and then peered at the top of a column of red granite 15-stories tall in the middle of the square. Instead of being dedicated to a Bolshevik hero, this monument named after Alexander I, the czar who defeated Napoleon in the winter of 1812, held a statue of an angel carrying a cross. That image burned in their minds and kept them going. Finally, the state granted them permission to visit the local *Society for Orphans.*

They shook with trepidation as they were led from room to room in the orphanage, which was housed in an abandoned school building.

Mr. Romanov, the chief custodian, searched for child # 543-31, whose weekly cost was calculated by meals served and soiled clothes cleaned. She and her husband entered a room and saw several girls, dressed in drab gray uniforms, 1 to 2 years old and one over 3 years old who had outgrown their crib.

The caretaker looked at the taller one and said, "We call her Natasha. Let me get her for you." He began putting on thin plastic gloves while saying, "We must be careful of germs and viruses…"

The sullen girl's bright eyes shone as someone needing love.

She rushed to the crib and lifted her out. The little girl clung to her. It was probably the first time Natasha had ever been hugged in that dreary place.

And now her daughter was here in this field house seeking redemption. They had already given her presents and helped her to recover. In a few days they would attend a church service and share a meal of baked ham trimmed with pineapple. They had no more money to spend on gifts, but maybe giving her a family was the greatest gift of all. Tears welled up in her eyes as her girl, beaming in a white leotard with blue trim, waved back to her.

***

The uneven bars loomed above, casting shadows on the floor mat. Even though Sophie was competing in the meet's first event, Natasha bowed her head, unable to imagine performing on that apparatus again this season. Serena led for the Wildcats. She looped around on the lower bar, lifting up her feet into a handstand, and smoothly transitioned to the high bar. She twirled around to gain speed and landed a one somersault dismount to score a 9.2.

Sophie was next. Natasha heard the other girls comment: "Good spin." "Her dismount is coming." Then, "No!"

Her score of 8.8. made all the girls cringe.

Finally, Charlotte was hoisted up to the high bar. The best athlete was always last. She moved from the high bar to low bar and back again with her body stretched out and her lines being elegant. Her flight element consisted of a forward layout with a full twist. When she stuck the landing, the new girls cheered. Her score…9.4.

The Titans went in-between the Wildcats and posted similar scores.

The girls marched over to the second rotation - the floor exercise. A Titans gymnast moved and tumbled to a Slavic dance by Dvorak. While she performed, Prudence hissed, “Chad, I need another towel.”

“I already gave you one,” he replied.

“Chad?”

“All right.” He scooted to a duffle bag and tossed her another towel. The girls on the bench giggled because they all knew that Prudence needed two towels - one to wipe her face and hands and the other to wipe the moisture off her stinky feet.

Prudence dipped her hands into a plastic tub of chalk and bathed her feet. The music had stopped so she stood next to the floor mat.

A judge raised a tiny green flag.

Prudence waved to the crowd and smiled. Her music started. Natasha didn’t want to watch her teammate, but the crowd’s ohs and ahs became contagious, drawing her eyes that way. Prudence propelled herself across the mat by using the strength in her shoulders to round off cartwheels into handsprings. She spun and tumbled until she was smack in the middle. Her routine ended by leaping straight up and bending into a forward layout with a triple twist. She slipped, but maintained her footing and held out her arms to show she had landed upright. Even so the judges scored it a 9.6.

Prudence stomped her foot and grimaced because she didn’t get a 9.7 or 9.8. Most of the girls on the team could only get a 9.3 or 9.4 if the judging was lenient. But she had become enraged with herself because of a small break in form.

Natasha was next. She slipped on her gymnast shoes and stood at the floor mat. When the judge raised the green flag, she held her hand up and took a deep breath. She dashed across the mat, tumbled, rolled, and leaped into the air. Landing a few feet short of the corner, she took several stiff-legged steps to reach it. The crowd clapped to the folk tune’s beat as she pranced along the mat’s edge and waved in a funky manner. Reaching the other corner, she squared herself. Then she tumbled to the mat’s center and spun in a circle until she formed a little ball. The music ended. A smattering of applause came from the stands.

Her score…9.1.

She sat on the bench and sighed with relief.

Robin, their specialist on this event, followed the last Titan. She leaped and rolled as though blasted from a cannon and bounced up in the corner. Squaring herself, the crowd fell silent. Then she tumbled in an acrobatic pass that left everyone's jaw hanging. She moseyed to the middle of the mat. She launched into a double Arabian - taking off backwards, turning a half twist, and doing a double front flip. When she stuck the landing, several fans popped up and cheered. Even Coach Jayne clapped.

Then the score came…9.9.

Coach Jayne shouted to the stone-faced judges, "What's wrong with that?"

"Nothing," replied Chad.

"They're not giving out 10s today," said the coach, tramping along the bench.

The vault was the meet's third event. Fans murmured with anticipation because of the high flying acrobatics they were about to see. A Titans teammate landed a one somersault vault in a tuck position, causing the crowd to cheer.

Even though Robin went last on the floor routine for the Wildcats, she readied herself for the vault by rubbing her hands and feet in chalk. She crouched down like a runner starting a 100-meter dash. She romped down the runway, hit the springboard with a whop, pushed off the table, and somersaulted twice. When she came down, a thud sounded as she stuck the landing. Wildcat supporters cheered from the stands. The girls bounced up from the bench and clapped. It earned a 9.6.

Katarina, the shortest Titan at 4'8" and the Wildcats toughest competitor, lined up. Her locks of brown hair were weaved behind her neck into a French braid to show off her face, and her squat build resembled a sparkplug. Even though she could barely see over the four-foot high table, she jogged down the mat. She did a round off, hit the springboard, and pushed off the table while increasing her speed and height. She catapulted through the air higher than the others, doing a double forward layout. The crowd erupted again despite an extra step on the landing. The judges awarded a 9.7.

Natasha's friend was up. Sophie jogged down the runway and banged into the springboard at an odd angle. Even so she twisted before hitting the table and pushing off. She somersaulted through the air and spun another half twist on the way down. Going sideways, she stuck out her arms to hold onto the landing. Her score…9.2.

She limped off the mat and stopped, holding her right foot up. Several girls lugged her back to the bench. Her eyes well up with tears, but she muffled any crying.

Chad wrapped a bandage around her knee. He advised the coach, "Select her replacement."

Coach Jayne peered at Natasha and then at Charlotte. She thought for a moment and called out, "Natasha, get ready for the balance beam."

The last Titan teammate had already gone. That girl was standing behind the vault waiting for her score…9.8. The crowd erupted again because the Titans were narrowing the Wildcats lead.

Prudence galloped down the runway, hit the springboard, and pushed off the table to get big air. She twisted three times and tucked her body in a forward layout position. When she landed, her momentum threatened to cause her to tumble.

She stuck out her right foot to hold onto the landing, but tread on one of the parallel boundary lines. Stepping to the side, she looked at the spot where she landed and twisted her face as though something was wrong with the floor mat. She waited for her score…9.4.

Prudence grunted and stomped her foot. She did not get the 9.6 or 9.7 she usually did. She came to the bench, took a sip from a water bottle, and tossed it aside. It rattled around her chair and came bouncing out on the floor.

Coach Jayne grabbed her and said, "Calm down."

Her heavy breathing subsided.

"Prudence, hold your head high," pleaded the coach. "We need you to focus on your final event. Can you do that?"

Prudence nodded. She picked up her water bottle and plopped in her seat.

The meet's most challenging event - the balance beam - was last. The Wildcats first competitor was Lynn. Since she was the shortest girl at 5'2" and had a low center of gravity, she maintained her balance with ease. While she treaded and tumbled across the beam, Coach Jayne kneeled in front of Natasha and said, "The Titans have pulled ahead. You need to get a 9 to keep us in the competition. Plant your feet on the beam before you do an element and make sure your forward handsprings are fluid." She walked away.

That was the team's style - to make sure all the movements were solid and not to try anything too dangerous. Natasha sighed. She had never gotten a 9 on the beam in her life. Her routine didn't have enough risky elements.

"Natasha, you can do it," insisted Sophie.

"I don't know," she mumbled.

Lynn scored a 9.4, which was a good mark. While the Titan's teammate did her routine, Natasha readied herself for the final event. She slipped off her gymnast shoes and chalked up her hands and feet. She decided to insert some moves into her routine that she practiced alone in the field house. It would have to come from a deeper place if she was to get that 9. She remembered clutching onto that music box and watching Olga Korbut perform on the beam. Could she perform elements that beautiful?

A 9.3 for the Titans gymnast caused more cheering to come from the stands because the defending champions still clung to the lead.

Natasha Fuller called out the elderly announcer.

Natasha stood by the beam and held up her hand to acknowledge the judges. She did a handstand on the beam, followed by a forward flip, beginning her routine with a bang. Peeking to the side, she saw Coach Jayne's mouth hanging open because she had already done the most difficult element she practiced with the team. She readied herself for the rest of her routine.

With a series of small jumps, Natasha made her way to the plank's midpoint. She kneeled down, placing her weight on one knee and holding the other leg straight out. She spun in a circle, 360 degrees, on the bent foot, a move usually reserved for the floor. She stood and stepped to the end of the beam. 16 feet of plank extended behind her. She raised both hands straight over her head and slowly bent backwards, arching her back to form a circle. Cameras flashed and teammates gasped. Every muscle in her body ached, but she wheeled round and round, performing two backward handsprings. Then she crouched down into a sitting position and leaped, doing an aerial back flip.

"Oh, Tasha!" uttered Sophie.

Her feet caught the beam, and she strained to keep from slipping off. More cameras clicked and flashed.

"Hold on!" gasped a girl from her bench.

A fall would mean an automatic one-point deduction. She tipped forward, trying to right herself. Her head was falling toward her waist. If she broke the plane, the judges would deduct three-tenths from her score. She held her hands out to maintain her form. Then she rose and waved in a funky manner as though that was part of her routine. She stepped backwards to the end of the beam.

Her dismount was next. Natasha lowered her arms and took a deep breath. She propelled herself with forward handsprings, end over end, down the plank. When she ran out of room, she bent her knees and bounced off the bar, holding onto a tight pike position while somersaulting once. Her feet hit the mat and she plummeted into a crouch. She stood straight up with her hands raised, sticking the landing.

Loud cheering came from the crowd.

She moved to the front of the mat. Her score…9.5.

She hesitated, afraid Coach Jayne would scold her for changing her routine. Instead, when she came off the floor, the coach patted her head and purred, "Good job, sweetie."

Natasha stumbled and pulled up. She limped to her seat with her left ankle aching. A couple girls hugged her.

"Tasha, you did it," said Sophie. "We're still in the meet."

"I did the best I could."

Chad came over and said, "Let me take a look." He placed ice packs on each side of her ankle and wrapped a bandage around her foot.

She had a slight sprain.

Chad returned to his usual spot and said, "I guess you didn't know she could do the Korbut Flip?"

"No, I didn't," replied Coach Jayne.

"It's the stubborn ones that improve," commented Chad.

"Yes," nodded the coach, "I've got two of them on my team."

Prudence chalked up her hands and feet. She squinted her eyes and looked at Natasha with disdain.

"Don't pay attention to her," said Sophie. "She's just psyching herself up."

The Titan's best gymnast, Katarina, anchored their event. The 4'8" dynamo mounted the beam by doing a backward handspring. She danced its length, *sur les pointes,* on tiptoes with her arms and hands fully extended, appearing to be a full foot taller. She knew no fear of heights because she was raised in the Carpathian foothills of Hungary, scooting from rock to rock on mountain trails with thousand foot drops. Her tumbling sequence consisted of four consecutive forward handsprings from end to end. Then she flung herself through the air and stuck a double forward somersault for the dismount. The judges' 9.8 got the crowd roaring.

"Damn!" yelped Coach Jayne. "I don't know if we can catch them."

"She's good enough for the nationals," said Chad.

Prudence looked at the judges with furrowed eyebrows, questioning their judgment. She stood next to the apparatus waiting.

"Come on, Prue," yelled Robin. "You can do it."

The gymnast did not hear her because she was locked in a trance, visualizing the movements of her routine ahead of time.

A judge raised the green flag.

Prudence mounted the beam and bounded backwards with two handsprings to the middle. Then she turned 360 degrees with one leg stretched out ballerina style. Though graceful she seemed off center.

"Did you see her wobble?" asked Natasha.

"What?" said Sophie.

Prudence became jaunty as she moved from one end of the beam to the other with her high leg kicks and bold arm swings defying gravity. She turned and wheeled end over end until she was doing a hand stand in the middle, spreading her legs apart to resemble the branches of a tree. Natasha knew that her arms must be burning and her back aching. The athlete wheeled upright and pranced with precision to the other end and spun around. She lowered her arms to the sides and took a deep breath to get ready for the dismount. Then it came.

Prudence twirled end over end without bending her knees or elbows...thunk...thunk... thunk...a propeller blade slicing across the beam's length. She bent her knees with only empty space before her and leaped through the air like a swimmer going off a springboard. She tucked her body, doing one somersault, while completing two and a half twists, becoming a blur. There was a loud thud, and she stood there on the floor mat with her arms raised toward the ceiling.

Applause erupted in the stands.

Chad screamed, "She stuck the landing!"

"Did you see anything wrong?" asked Coach Jayne.

"No, I didn't see any mistakes." Chad kneeled on the floor and scanned the scores through all of the events performed that evening. "If that is good enough to get a 9.9, the teams are tied."

The audience went hush, waiting for the judges to announce the score.

"Robin and Lynn," yelled Coach Jayne, "get ready for your vaults. There's going to be a playoff." She turned to Chad and said, "Make sure they have what they need."

He scurried around to get their shoes and chalk for a tiebreaking playoff.

Prudence stood on the floor waiting for her score. Then it came.

"10," screamed Coach Jayne.

All the girls yelled and ran toward her.

Prudence held her arms out and leaned in a backwards bow, soaking up the applause and roars from the crowd. The girls lifted her up and carried her around inside the field house. All the while Natasha was stuck on the bench icing her injured ankle. Prudence held up the championship trophy as students joined in a procession around the oval. The team pumped their fists as they entered their dressing room.

Chad helped Natasha get to the dressing room. Inside the girls shouted and laughed. They gathered around Prudence, taking selfies with the gymnast and trophy. The coach came over to Natasha and asked, "How's your ankle?"

"Better."

"Tape it up before you board the bus. I'll be back to help you." She disappeared behind a row of lockers. "Let me get in here," said Coach Jayne. "Let me take another one." She was taking selfies with Prudence and the trophy too.

The girls showered, got dressed, and left to board the bus. Natasha sponged off her body, dressed, and wrapped her sprained ankle. At least she competed, she thought. She didn't come close to winning any events, but she was a gymnast again. Maybe that was the real reward of her ordeal.

Natasha was alone, listening to water dripping from the faucets in the shower room. She heard the clopping of sneakers on the moist tile floor on the other side of the lockers. Then the clopping came toward her. A shadow engulfed her as Prudence stood nearby.

The gymnast looked down and said, "My 10 would not have meant anything if you didn't get that 9.5. You and I gave the school a nice Christmas present."

"Do you think so?"

"You saw and heard them when I was carried around the field house."

"I did."

"I shouldn't have gotten that 10," admitted Prudence. "I wobbled on the 360."

"I know."

"I kept the motion going to fool the judges. If you would keep your momentum when you make a mistake, you could probably get a tenth to two-tenths more on each routine."

"Are you sure?"

"Yeah," she nodded. "You're a good gymnast."

"Thank you."

"I've seen you in my English Lit class," said Prudence. "They say those classic authors like Dickens and Austen could turn a phrase to give a story a good ending, but I don't know much about them."

"I have trouble with English Lit too," replied Natasha.

"Some of us study at Thompson Hall," stated Prudence. "We meet on Thursdays at 3:30 p.m. on the second floor overlooking the pond. Would you like to join us?"

"Sure, I can do that."

"Cool." Prudence turned and trotted toward the door.

Natasha watched the girl with the slender frame, masculine shoulders, and legs as powerful as a thoroughbred. That was her rival, training partner, spotter, tormentor, nemesis, and now friend.

From the Top of the World

Hector felt good striding into the fast food restaurant where everything was so clean because his clothes were giving off a sharp odor after working so hard. He was hungry enough to eat there, but would leave with everyone else after they received their orders. The first time they tried to eat there the gringo manager asked them to leave, raising such a ruckus they thought that ICE (U.S. Immigration and Customs Enforcement) would swoop down on them. Some of his coworkers didn't have green cards and screamed in Spanish, "Let us go, quick." "We can hide at the construction site." Several refused to come back. Hector's knees ached today. He wobbled several times while shuffling across the steel girders because the wind whipped by so hard.

He spotted a dressed up fart standing in another line at the counter. A guy who had probably never done a hard day of work in his life. The only honest work is done with your bare hands the way God intended. Namby-pambies who shuffle papers around on a desk are not working. Though a few of those people were needed to process the paperwork on the building they were putting up.

Hector ordered a cheeseburger and fries. The burgers were always juicy there and the fries salted just right. The salt had a sweet taste he couldn't get enough of. The waitress lady behind the counter said, "That will be six dollars seventy-eight cents." She had a cute face for a gringa and was dressed up in a dandy blue & white uniform. He felt so proud when he pulled out that big ten dollar bill, which was engraved with a picture of Hamilton looking like a religious icon, and gave it to her. Hamilton was a famous American president or somebody like that. When he first came to this country he would look at the pictures of those famous Americans. Washington, Jefferson, Grant, Lincoln. Men who shaped the country into what it is today: a land of freedom and opportunity.

His sister, Cassandra, immigrated a year after he did, but has studied American history a lot more and desires to become a citizen. She wants to marry an American who was born here. She likes men in fancy suits and ties like that namby-pamby at the counter. Perhaps she can find happiness here away from the poverty of their former home in Tijuana.

***

The Excel Caterers could not deliver lunch to a lot of their customers that day because more than half their staff had called out sick with the flu. Lloyd received a text message saying that only prestigious events taking place at local hotels were being catered. That meant he had to endure the insult of riding the elevator down to the lobby and rubbing elbows with the common folk at lunch hour. It was bad enough when tourists gawked through shop windows at souvenirs such as coffee cups or T-shirts with a skipjack or a crab printed on them, but it was getting close to Christmas and shops now sported displays of Santa Clauses, reindeer, and evergreen trees. Those out-of-town fools formed knots on the sidewalk he had to detour around. They didn't realize the holiday season was just a gimmick used by businesses to boost sales.

Lloyd looked through the windows of eateries along the street. What he saw and smelled upset him: clouds of steam spreading along the ceilings of cafés and strange odors escaping out of their front doors. And he could see spots of grease splattered on the aprons of waiters and waitresses. He couldn't believe anybody would serve food under these unsanitary conditions or that the cafes hadn't already been closed down by the health department. Then he spotted a fast food restaurant encased in a steel and plastic shell that looked spic-and-span from the outside. He peered through the window and saw a clerk wiping off a table. He stepped inside, strode up to the counter, and studied the menu hanging down from the ceiling. Overwhelmed by the options, he simply stated what he wanted, "I'll have a beef patty with melted cheddar cheese and a slice of tomato. Also, serve me a Coke."

The clerk turned her head and shouted, "Number 2, no lettuce." She poked a couple cartoon pictures on the cash register because mathematics, even basic arithmetic, was probably too complex for this graduate of the local school system. She looked up and yapped, "Six dollars and twenty-three cents."

Lloyd handed her the gold card from his billfold.

"Sorry, sir, we don't take credit cards for purchases less than ten dollars."

"Let me speak to the manager."

"Sarah, I need your help," the clerk squealed.

An older woman with gray hair and an "assistant manager" pin on her uniform came forward. She saw the credit card in Lloyd's hand. "Didn't she tell you we won't take that."

"I told him," said the clerk.

Lloyd looked baffled. He slipped the gold card, with its $75,000 credit limit, back into his wallet. Cash. He couldn't remember the last time he held a bill in his hands. A swipe of a pass key or credit card had been good enough for years. Now this indignity. He began searching for the bill he kept in case of an emergency, but it had been so long since he saw it. He couldn't remember what fold of leather it was hidden underneath. The clerk had an impatient look on her face. He heard grumbling behind him. Then he found it behind his Country Club membership card. A hundred dollar bill. He handed it to the clerk.

She opened the cash drawer and her chin dropped. She whined, "Do you have anything smaller?"

Lloyd placed a hand on his hip and snapped, "Miss, I expect my change right now."

"Sarah," yodeled the clerk, "I need your help again."

The assistant manager raced around the food bins.

"He gave me this."

The assistant manager pulled a bank bag from underneath the cash register and counted out the change: $93.77. The coins felt heavy and odd in his hand. He plunked them down on the counter. The clerk poured him a Coke, sealed the cup with a plastic lid, and dashed back.

He couldn't believe he was being served by this snotty clerk with the oblong head. She said, "The waiting line is over there."

Now he had to stand to one side while a parade of customers ordered food. At another cash register there was a knot of messy construction workers jabbering in a foreign gibberish. His secretary, Sandra, was Hispanic, but he didn't know from what country. And she never spoke in that strange lingo. She used refined English that was peppered with business acronyms. This was too much too bear. "Miss," he huffed, "I've been waiting here for over five minutes."

"Where's the number 2, no lettuce!" yelled the clerk.

"Coming up!" A kid who looked like he was fresh out of high school with a goofy grin on his baby-face flipped the burger into a white bag and hustled forward. "Here."

Lloyd felt like roaring into the clerk's ear, but the damn woman was off again bagging fries for another customer. Then hunger began gnawing at his stomach.

Lloyd sat at a table by the window. He unfolded a paper napkin on his lap and squeezed more ketchup onto his burger from a plastic packet. He shook his head in disbelief at these items. When the Excel Caterers brought lunch into his office, they supplied cotton napkins and bottles of condiments. He ate while children scampered around him, mothers screamed at their kids, teenagers played a video game that pinged and made crash noises each time they moved the joysticks, and pop music blasted out of speakers above him. He was glad when he left. On the walk back to his office he made sure not to get his slacks wet on the piles of snow melting on the curbs. He rode the elevator back up to his floor and settled into the leather chair behind his mahogany desk.

His secretary, Sandra, was eating a salad for lunch. Her desk was in the middle of the floor next to the copier and fax machine. Sandra's skin looked like it was being bathed in the fading sunlight at dusk and her long, straight black hair had a bluish tint as though it had been brushed with a comb made from sapphire.

"How's our bronze goddess doing today?" His buddy, Jeffrey, was straddling the office doorway. "Same dress as yesterday. Probably got laid last night. What a terrific body. Why don't you make a move on her?"

"You know why!"

"Isn't Amy out of town?"

"For two weeks," said Lloyd with a pout. "She's doing a photo shoot in L.A."

"Then go for it. That woman can tide you over for a couple weekends."

Walt plodded by and poked his head into the office, "The Old Man is looking for you."

"Tell him I'll be there in 10 minutes," said Lloyd.

"I saw her coming out of the Bahamas Club last Friday," said Jeffrey. "That's probably where she meets them. You could…"

Lloyd was gathering papers together.

"…You're not listening?"

"I got to get ready for this meeting. We're closing a deal with Capital Savings & Loan."

"If I was you…" Jeffrey winked, then walked away.

Sandra held her head down while she ate. She felt ashamed to be wearing the same plain dress that she had worn yesterday. She felt ashamed to be poor. If her coworkers knew that she had lived in a shanty town on the outskirts of Tijuana, they would probably shun her. That was why she was glad to be living on the East Coast. If she had moved to California, then someday someone would say they had seen her selling trinkets on the side of the highway. They would make fun of her and laugh. She munched on the salad. Since moving to this country, she had trouble keeping the weight off. She always fixed her brother, Hector, a large dinner of tacos - corn tortillas stuffed with grilled meat and cheese or her specialty, Cordero Jalisco, tender lamb slow-baked in banana leaves and simmered in chili sauce. Sometimes, she'd even make Arroz con pollo, a dish of seasoned chicken served with rice, sweet peas, and roasted peppers. And she capped each meal with a tasty dessert such as custard flan or sopapilla, a mound of fried dough smeared with honey. Nothing was too good for him. Hector was courageous enough to come to this country and get a good job. He sent her money to travel here. Now he was providing a roof over her head.

Jeffrey was right, thought Lloyd. Why shouldn't he have a little fun? Amy was going to be out of town for a while and when she came back she would probably be too tired to do anything. He peered out of the window on the 25th floor. The skyscraper rose above the noise and ruckus of the city. Its interior was ultra-clean, more sanitary than a hospital but without the jarring smell of ammonia. His office had a plush white carpet and was equipped with the latest computer gadgetry. And he made enough money to buy suits made with a blend of silk and wool that felt as comfortable as pajamas. He looked at the streets below and realized he didn't have to become tangled up in mundane problems such as fixing a flat tire or dealing with store clerks across a counter because everything could be solved with a cell phone and credit card. The same with Sandra. The woman would wither as soon as the barrage began. He pulled out his black book and thumbed to *florists*. Under each florist was a list of their special bouquets including the following: yellow daffodils with a card that read *Flowers to brighten your day, the way you brighten mine*, eleven red roses with the quote *There are only eleven because you make twelve*, a cluster of white orchids *None of these are as beautiful as you*... Then he found it. The perfect bouquet. He dialed that florist.

An hour passed before the delivery man sauntered onto the floor wearing a khaki jacket with the words *Hillcrest Farm* engraved in lime-green on the front pocket. He set the plastic pot and flowers wrapped in gold foil on the corner of her desk. "You're Sandra. The one I'm looking for."

"Excuse me, sir."

"The flowers are for *Sandra*."

"Let me search the phone directory." Sandra scanned through the book for an employee whose first name was the same as hers.

"The card says it's for Sandra Ramirez."

"That is me." She was stunned. Who would send her flowers? It was not her birthday or any special occasion. And her brother, Hector, would never waste money on such an extravagance.

The man stood there and held out his hand.

She did not have enough money to buy food or soft drinks from a vending machine much less tip him. She only managed to muster, "Thank you…much."

The man stalked off muttering a few profane words.

She peeled away the gold foil to reveal a lush bouquet of pink roses. The note on the little card thrilled her: *You make the loveliest part of my day*. It was from Lloyd, one of her bosses. The man with the blonde crew cut who sat in the corner office. Around her he always acted so analytical and professional, but deep down inside he must be a naive boy. Why else this impulsive act?

Another secretary, Caroline, stooped over the flowers and drew in a whiff. She picked up the card and put it down again. "You have to watch that one."

Sandra was not sure what that meant. She was not familiar enough with English to know that Caroline was giving her a warning. Instead, she thought that *watching someone* would be something you do at the beach when you saw a muscular man wading out of the water with nothing on but his swimming trunks.

Lloyd closed the deal. The bank would acquire the mortgage lender from Philadelphia by purchasing its shares at a $6 dollar premium. Moving the assets around on the balance sheet would require the rest of the afternoon. The numbers were still running through his head when he saw Sandra. It was time to close his next deal. He strolled over to her desk. "I hope you like the flowers."

"Yes, Mr. Miller," said Sandra. "I am flattered you would do such a thing."

"It's nothing at all. You have been working here for a month so it's about time we get to know each other." He gazed into her almond-shaped eyes. The fluorescent light bounced off her black pupils the way starlight would be reflected off a dark pool of water. He lost his concentration for a moment, then said, "If you're not busy this evening, I could take you to a nice restaurant in Little Italy. Would you like that?"

"Yes, Mr. Miller. That would be fine."

"I'll meet you in the lobby at 5:30."

She watched him walk back to his office. She wondered what it would be like to go out with a gringo. She had thought about it when she lived in Tijuana, but knew her mother would not allow it. Up here everything was different. She had to make her own life. She called her brother and left a message that she had to work late. He would understand that. They were many times Hector would put in extra hours to make sure he did not lose his job.

Lloyd strutted back to his office feeling supreme confidence. Sandra was stupid enough to fall for the bouquet - hook, line and sinker. All he had to do was lead her into shallow water and scoop her up with a net. It cost him $357 dollars to catch Amy. He sent her flowers, fed her a meal at Valentino's, took her to a show at the Hippodrome, and topped it off with a romantic horse carriage ride along the harbor. That was his typical routine. But he wouldn't have to blow a big wad of cash on this one. He could probably skip the show and horse carriage ride. This woman reflected her station in life. She was only a secretary pretending to be something more.

At 5 p.m. employees rushed to the elevators. Only a few remained behind to tidy up their desks. Sandra put away the files she had worked on and rode the elevator down. She waited in the lobby and counted off the minutes. When the flow of people had ebbed to a trickle, the doors of an elevator clacked open and Lloyd stepped out cocooned in a black overcoat and black gloves made of lamb skin. "Are you ready, Hon'?" He strolled out the revolving door. She followed.

Snowflakes swirled around them and danced in the air. A chill stung their faces. Sandra's teeth chattered. Lloyd looped his arm around her. "Being outside is like being a popsicle in a freezer…"

"Yes, Mr. Miller, the air is cold."

"…and you, Sandra, must be the sweetest one because you smell so good."

"Thank you, Mr. Miller. I wash my hair every morning."

"Please call me Lloyd."

"Yes, Lloyd."

"It's more than that, Sandra. Everything about you smells so sweet."

They hiked down the hill toward the harbor. Lloyd ushered her into a store selling women's clothing. He led her over to a counter. "Let me buy you a scarf. It's the least I can do on an evening like this."

There was a display of wool and cashmere scarves in every color. Sandra picked through them until she found one she liked. Lloyd bought it for her. She flung the red scarf around her neck and let one end hang down on either side of her green coat, the solid blocks of color being cheerful like the season. As they strolled toward Little Italy, she leaned her head against his shoulder. She was melting.

Valentino's was located in a remodeled brick townhouse. The tuxedo-clad maître d', Antonio, waved them in. He was a stout gentleman with a thin moustache and olive complexion. He led them to a table decked with a baby blue cloth and set with sparkling silverware. The restaurant's ceiling was high, but a fireplace kept the dining room warm. Their waiter was a tall, skinny lad named Tito who spoke little English and indicated he understood their orders by a simple nod. He had only been in this country for a few months and still longed to be scooting around the cobblestone streets of Sicily.

Antonio soon returned cradling a dark green bottle in his arms. "You will like this, Mr. Miller. Chardonnay Le Bruniche from Tuscany." He popped the cork and filled their glasses to the brim with a dry white wine. While they waited for their order, they listened to violin music played by an old gentleman with a wrinkled face and distinguished gray sideburns. Giuseppe moved from table to table and swayed this way and that. One moment a wonderful operatic aria floated from the strings; the next it sounded as though a schoolboy was sawing a musical scale. But this was fine because Valentino's was strictly a family affair with members of an extended Italian family performing all of the functions from cook to maître d'.

They nibbled on appetizers of shrimp renato broiled in a light wine sauce and topped with melted mozzarella cheese and fresh honeydew melon draped with thin slices of prosciutto ham; shoveled down delicious bites of lasagna layered with ricotta and mozzarella cheeses and veal cacciatore simmered in a homemade marinara sauce sprinkled with mushrooms and green peppers; and stuffed themselves for dessert with cannolis, pastry rolls stuffed with a creamy sweet filling.

During dinner Lloyd told her how he earned a MBA in Finance from the Wharton School in Pennsylvania and accepted a job with the bank. Once there he advanced from one department to another. He made it sound very innocent and harmless. He didn't tell her how he helped to build a financial empire whose pipeline of products reached into everybody's pocket with banking and ATM fees, double digit credit card interest rates, auto loan and mortgage payments, investment commissions, health and life insurance premiums, and retirement account administrative charges that sucked the money out like a vacuum cleaner. Then he summed up his current financial status, "My father always says, *If you pinch the pennies, the dollars will take care of themselves.*"

Sandra was enamored from the beginning. She had never eaten in a restaurant so plush with a legion of busboys and waiters scurrying from table to table. The only place she and Hector would go was the local sub shop where they fixed your food in an assembly line fashion and did not have enough tables for all of their customers. This man across from her, besides being so clean cut, must also love his family dearly. Wasn't that what she wanted? To start a family with a successful man like that?

After dinner they wandered along the harbor with their arms wrapped around each other and listened to waves lapping against the bulwark and seagulls squawking overhead while wheeling in the darkened sky. Yachts were anchored at the marina with their lights twinkling brighter than stars. Other couples walked hand in hand enjoying the same scenery.

They stopped at Lombard Street. He hailed a cab that had an evergreen wreath with a red bow fastened on its front grill. A heavyset black man got out and opened the rear door. "Ma'am'." Sandra slid into the back seat, impressed with how fast the car stopped. "Sir." Lloyd followed.

The driver settled into the front seat upon a liner of beads that massaged his sore back while he drove. He spoke with a British accent, "Where may I take you?"

Lloyd glanced at the driver's license hooked to the front shade. The name read: Addo Kwabena. "Addo, take us to Fells Point. The address is…"

Sandra felt so comfortable she blurted out her address.

They were going back to her place. This woman would be easier to get into bed than he thought. She was caught in his net.

"Addo, where are you from?" inquired Sandra.

"From Nigeria, ma'am," replied the driver. "Been living in this country for four years." He recited his history of employment with different cab companies.

Soon they were cruising down Sandra's street. Several townhouses had paint peeling off windowsills and cracks in the cement steps leading up to the front door. Her house had a stucco facade and white blinds covering the windows. Lloyd let the driver swipe his gold card on a portable credit card machine and add a five dollar tip.

"Both of you," yelled Addo, "have a Merry Christmas."

Lloyd held her around the waist as she unlocked the front door. The rooms were painted in earthy colors of yellow and brown. A television was playing in the living room. A short fellow got up from the sofa. Did this woman have children? That would spoil everything.

"Lloyd, I would like you to meet my brother, Hector."

Lloyd couldn't believe he was shaking the hand of this runt. The fellow had no more class than a skid row bum. His hair was wild and unkempt, a red rash or abrasion covered one cheek, an odor came from his dirt-stained shirt, and he spoke in a broken English that made it sound like he had marbles in his mouth. He would have to get rid of him to be alone with Sandra.

What did his sister see in this guy? Every time Hector looked at his smug face he winced. Was this namby-pamby waiting for an orchestra to play Beethoven? Was he planning to pick up knitting needles to darn a pair of socks? The guy even wore color-coordinated clothes the way a woman would with the maroon handkerchief in his front jacket pocket matching his maroon shirt. This namby-pamby had dainty hands with pink fingers. Not the calloused hands and cracked skin of a man who knew how to do an honest day of work. Not hands smeared with grease or discolored by a chemical handled during the day. Not hands that were swollen up to one and a half times their size because of the pounding they took when you bolted or hammered something together. But dainty hands with pink fingers. Hector could only mutter his disbelief and shake his head.

They sauntered into the living room and sat down. Sandra opened a drawer on the side table and took out a box of wooden matches. "Lloyd, would you honor us by lighting a candle this holiday season? It is a tradition started by my mother, Isabella. Hector and myself would be most pleased."

"A what?" Lloyd couldn't believe anybody was so stupid. The entire holiday season was a scam started by department stores to sell merchandise, but he would play along if that was what Sandra wanted. "Sure, Hon', why not?"

Sandra handed Lloyd the match.

He felt stupid lighting a candle in a plastic holder shaped like a boat. He didn't believe in this religious nonsense. Nobody knew whether there was a God or not. So you may as well make as much money as you can and spend it. That was the only way to be happy. He scraped the match against the box and it came alive with a puff of acrid smoke. He touched the wick with the flame and lit the candle. He wanted to make Sandra happy and come one step closer to making love to her.

Sandra bowed her head when Lloyd passed the flame to her. This was a time-honored tradition in the Ramirez household: the lighting of scented candles. Her brother found the candlestick holder in a trash heap with the end broken off. So instead of holding five candles, it only held three. If they did not take it, someone else would. Nothing of value found in the trash went to waste because a needy family was always ready to use it. She would honor this tradition because she wanted to appease God and Pope Francis. She would pray for peace in the world when she attended Christmas mass. She let the flame pass to the second candle. A warm feeling filled her chest.

Hector received the flame from his sister. It felt good to be in the same household with her. He had invited their mother to come to America, but the old woman wanted to stay close to her husband's grave. He could not understand the sentimentality of women. Perhaps he never would. Sandra was the only family he had. He stretched out his arm, careful not to touch the base with the flame. He knew the candlestick holder was not silver, but only an imitation made of pewter and painted a glossy color. The coating was flammable. He lit the wick of the third candle. Now the entire room glowed.

Lloyd pulled the dark green bottle from his overcoat pocket. It was still half full after dinner so he snatched it. He poured the wine into clay mugs that Sandra brought out from the kitchen. He wanted to snuggle up to her, but her brother sat on a chair across from the sofa with his eyes darting from him to Sandra and back again. The last time Lloyd had a chaperon was at a birthday party when he was twelve years old, but he still managed to sneak Darlene Williams into the closet underneath the stairs and French kiss her. He would have to dispatch this runt.

Hector guzzled his cup of wine and murmured something agreeable about the vino blanco.

Lloyd shook the bottle. A sloshing sound came from the bottom. "We're running a bit low. We'll need another bottle."

"Lloyd, this is enough," said Sandra. "We all have to work tomorrow."

"Tomorrow is a long time away, my sweet darling." Lloyd pulled out his cell phone and dialed a number. "Antonio, this is Lloyd Miller. Pull another bottle of the Chardonnay LeBruniche. I'm sending someone to pick it up. Uh-huh. He'll be there before you close." He snapped his fingers, "Hector, come over here."

The runt responded to his demand.

"Go down to Valentino's in Little Italy and ask for Antonio. He will give you a bottle to bring back. Try a cannoli while you're there." Lloyd pulled out his billfold. He still had the $93 in change from lunch. He pulled out a $50 bill and gave it to Hector. The runt could only bob his head up and down and say gracias over and over again like the fool he was. Lloyd topped off Sandra's wine glass as Hector put on his jacket and hopped out the door.

Lloyd had a history of seduction learned from trial and error, stretching from his teenage days when he took his high school sweetheart to their senior prom through his turb lent 20s when every fling was a sporting event to his 30s when he wowed them with sophistication. He knew that the wine had to be chilled, the music contemporary, and the atmosphere inside dark and cozy. He could hang on to every word they said and deliver compliments with a straight face even though each one was a bold lie. He started out wimpy and unsure of himself, but now could sweep any woman into bed with one gallant gesture after another, always ending in a slow peeling off of clothes. The time had come for conquest. He leaned closer. "You are as beautiful as a summer day."

"Me…bonita?"

"Yes, you are bonita." He kissed her moist lips and placed his hand on her knee.

She grabbed his wrist.

He rolled on top of her and slid his hand along the inside of her thigh.

Sandra knew what he wanted. She had seen stray dogs humping each other in the trash-strewn alley behind her family's shack in Tijuana. She was not a dog. She was a God-fearing woman who believed in His wrath. A wrath that would bring her bad luck if she sinned. She did not want to beg for forgiveness in a confession booth at Saint Elizabeth's Church. She pushed him back.

Lloyd wasn't about to let this woman squirm away. She was already drowsy from the wine. All he had to do was get her hot and he could take anything he wanted. He pinned her against the armrest.

"Hector! Hector!" she yelped.

She grunted under his weight. All he could think of were the rhythmic moans of love making that would soon be coming from her mouth. He did not hear Hector making his way back into the house, jabbering to his sister, "Esta nevando. Necesito un a capucha." Or feel Hector's eyes burning into his back or feel the floorboards vibrate as he plodded toward him.

"Huh!?" Lloyd felt himself being lifted. His shoulders were slammed against the wall. He flailed his arms, but couldn't get away. The runt was standing in front of him like a raging bull. One hand was pushing on his chest. The other had a firm grip on his shirt collar. Lloyd flipped open his cell phone. "Unhand me or I'll call the police."

"Hector! Hector!" yelled Sandra again. This time she grabbed one of her brother's arms and pleaded with him to move away.

Hector grunted, then stepped back.

Lloyd flopped onto the sofa. A couple buttons had popped off his shirt. "Are you crazy?

This shirt cost me $80."

"Lo siento. Lo siento," said Sandra.

"You better be sorry," said Lloyd.

"My brother does not understand, Mr. Miller. Sometimes he gets angry."

Lloyd buttoned the cuff of one sleeve. The other sleeve flapped loosely because of a missing button. He slipped on his gray jacket and black overcoat. He loomed near them and spoke to Sandra, "I didn't do anything you didn't want me to. Then your brother did this. If I was you, I would start looking for another job."

Hector had enough. If he had not come back for his hat, something awful would have happened to his sister. Now this blonde-haired namby-pamby with the pale skin was threatening her again. "We go outside…man to man."

"No, Hector, por favor." Sandra got in-between them. "Mr. Miller, please go."

They were still jabbering to themselves when Lloyd stepped outside into the falling snow. He couldn't believe what peasants these people were. He was a man of education and wealth, but they had treated him like this. He knew he would do everything in his power to get that woman fired.

Cassandra collapsed in her brother's arms and sobbed. Hector now realized how brutal some Americans could be. How rude and insulting. Sure, there were great Americans who had built this country. There were also jerks tearing it down. Her sister's boss was one of those. Hector didn't know what to say to her. He stroked her silky hair as tears formed rivers that trickled down her cheeks.

***

The next morning Hector's work boots smacked across the kitchen floor while his sister's footsteps were a soft patter. Their routine had become so familiar that they spun out of each other's way automatically. His sister brewed a pot of coffee and poured some into a thermos for him while he raided the refrigerator and gobbled down leftovers for breakfast. Then he picked up his thermos and simply said, "Hasta lvego."

Hector didn't feel any remorse for what he had done. If he had done nothing, his sister would have been raped. He had seen a lot of things in America and not all of them were good. Sometimes he wished he was still living in Tijuana, but a lot of jobs were here and recruiters urged men like him to come north.

When he got to the construction site, trucks loaded with steel girders where lined around the block. He stepped into a wire cage and was hoisted up as far as it went. He shuffled out to the edge of the steel frame, sat down, and lit a cigarette. His legs were hanging over a steel girder, but he wasn't scared. He had been on this job since the beginning. He had seen the skyscraper rise from its moorings sunk in the ground to the 16th floor where he now was. The work was always the same. First they inserted vertical beams into the slots so it looked like a giant pitchfork sticking up in the air. Then a crane hoisted up four or five steel girders which dangled overhead and twisted in the wind, resembling a giant mobile. Hector clambered up the rungs of a ladder leaning against a vertical beam and caught an I-beam as it spun in his direction. He pulled bolts out of his pocket and riveted the steel girder to a vertical beam with the rapid whine of a power drill. Then he hoisted himself up. In a sitting position he humped along the I-beam toward another vertical beam on the building's edge. The crane operator moved the other end into place and Hector riveted it there. Each floor was made up of twenty vertical beams and forty-three I-beams laid out in a grid pattern. Other workers would come to lay down sheets of metal and pour the concrete. But Hector was always in the initial wave of construction workers. The ones who could lose their lives with a slip of the hand or a stumble. As he looked at the other skyscrapers emerging downtown, he got a sense of deep satisfaction because this sprawling city was being built by people just like him: Latino immigrants at the top of the world.

When the World Stops

Keith's shoes sunk into a snow pile that hadn't melted from the last storm as he crept from tree to tree and bush to bush to keep from being seen. The town's new residents had already put up their Christmas lights because the weather after Thanksgiving was warm for a spell. He couldn't understand why they did that. The families living in his apartment building couldn't afford to replace a light bulb inside their home much less put up colorful decorations. Even so he wanted to take a closer look to see how the yuppies lived. Fallen leaves crunched underneath his feet as the crisp night air encircled him.

When he got to the brand-new townhouses, Christmas lights shined through large patio windows in back. In most homes the curtains were drawn open while in others the lacey window shades were thin enough to see through. One living room contained a silver Christmas tree which held fire engine-red ornaments. In another home candles were lit on a dining room table that was set with crystal serving bowls that glistened. He wondered what type of celebration they were having. The next few houses contained nothing unusual.

A throaty ruff came from a beagle that pressed its snout against a glass sliding door. It lifted its head and howled.

Keith scampered behind a bush and ducked down. He waited until the dog's howling tailed off before he snuck behind another home, which had four large stockings pinned to a fireplace mantel. That family must have small children waiting for Santa to come. The next home had a string of colored lights fastened around the patio window but a bare evergreen inside. He decided to go back to the home with the fancy stuff on the dining room table.

Making a wide arc through the backyards, Keith crept toward that townhouse again. He tripped on the cement porch and smacked into a trellis, which trembled. A flower pot slipped off and fell before he could catch it. Crash. He scooped up the broken pieces and put them in his pocket. Then he leaned backwards for a moment and held his breath. He didn't want to make a sound. Even the breeze had died down and stopped rustling the fallen leaves. When he peeked inside, the woman acted surprised while the man, still wearing a white shirt from work, appeared calm. Keith was sure the evidence of his mishap was out of sight. The couple went back to setting the table. He could see a beef roast and a dish made with sliced potatoes. He inched closer to get a better look.

"Got you!" sounded a deep voice as someone's hands yanked on his jacket collar and grabbed his trousers.

Keith tried to twist away, whining, "I wasn't doing nothing."

"I'm Officer Wilkins," declared the man with the deep voice. "We're going to find out what you were doing." He spoke into a walkie-talkie, "I got the prowler, 10-70."

The dispatcher's voice crackled with static, "Do you need back-up?"

"No, code 4." Officer Wilkins now had a grip on Keith's belt and dragged him around to the front of the house.

"That's him!" yelped the woman hiding behind the well-dressed man, who stood in the doorway. "He looks like a junkie."

Keith's long brown hair fell over his eyes. He looked down at his gangly body and long arms, but didn't see anything unusual.

"That's the peeping Tom," reaffirmed the man. "He's been casing our home for a break-in. We just bought a new entertainment console and notebook computers."

"I'm not doing nothing," said Keith.

"Where do you live?" asked Officer Wilkins.

"Across the street."

The residents looked across the wide boulevard at a cement structure six stories high. Their mouths fell open when they realized this youth came from the "housing project."

"I'll be back in a moment." Officer Wilkins pushed him over to the patrol car and padded him down. After setting the broken flower pot pieces on its hood, the policeman got Keith's full name and address and placed him in the back seat behind a mesh screen.

Keith peeped through the holes in the screen, wondering if the earth was no longer rotating, and heard his breath seething out of him. He saw Officer Wilkins rapping with the residents and filling out a police report. He couldn't imagine what strange stories they were telling about him. He watched the policeman walking back to the patrol car. Officer Wilkins opened the rear door and ordered, "Get out!"

Keith rolled out of the seat and stood up. He saw his mom, who was shaped like a large pear with sloping shoulders and a bulge at the hips, shuffling down the sidewalk. She had no makeup on her face to cover the deep creases around her eyes and her short brown hair was unwashed, making it appear greasy and dirty.

"That's my brat!" shouted his mom. "What do you want to say to the man?"

"I ain't got nothing to say," retorted Keith, glaring at the home owner.

A whack sounded as his mom slapped his face. "Go on!"

"I'm sorry," said Keith, feeling the sting on his cheek. "I won't look through your window again."

"What else?" demanded his mom, holding a hand on her hip.

"I'll...I'll pay for any damage."

"Besides the flower pot," said the man's wife. "My roast is ruined and the other dishes are cold. We'll have to throw them away."

"Buy us another dinner," demanded the man, "or we'll file charges."

"He'll pay for your dinner," said his mom. "Send us a bill."

"Then that's it," stated Officer Wilkins. "I'll hold onto this police report until everything is settled. If I hear from Mr. Merritt again, I'll charge your son with 594, malicious mischief, and 488, petty theft."

A week went by without any word from the disgruntled residents of the new townhouse, making Keith think he was in the clear. Then on a Friday evening while he was watching television, the doorbell rang again and again. His mom got up from the sofa, saying, "I'm coming." The ringing kept up until she yanked open the door.

"I'm Glenn Merritt," said a well-dressed man. "This is a bill from Tidbit's Bistro. It's for the dinner your son spoiled."

His mom looked at a paper containing a photocopy of the bill and asked, "You got two bottles of wine?"

"He ruined my wife's birthday," sneered Mr. Merritt. "I made it up to her the best I could. Are you going to pay it or what?"

Keith didn't like the idea of a smart aleck in a suit sticking it to him, but his mom replied, "$516 is a lot of money, but he'll pay it. Is $25 a week all right?"

"Yes, but we'll be watching him. I gave the original to Officer Wilkins."

After his mom closed the door, Keith grumbled, "Mom, throw that away."

"You got your whole life ahead of you," she said. "I don't want you starting out with a criminal record."

"Oh, mom," he whined. "How am I going to pay this?"

"By working after school and on weekends. That's what I did when I was your age. It's time for you to become a man."

The next day Keith walked a mile to the shopping mall, which was shaped like a giant horseshoe with the smaller retail stores sandwiched in-between two department stores that anchored either side. He had been to the mall before and seen plenty of *Now Hiring* and *Help Wanted* signs. He peered into a window and saw his reflection: a plaid shirt, jeans, and dungaree jacket a bit worn out and dusty; hair flowing in all directions and hanging behind his neck like a horse's mane; and narrowed eyelids to look like an outlaw who had been riding on the trail for a long time. He was ready to ramble. He started at one end and decided to keep going until he was offered a job.

Shop owners and store managers did not greet him with enthusiasm. The Korean man at the dry cleaners jabbered in a foreign language and shooed him out, the middle-aged lady in charge of the food mart jeered, "We only hire applicants with experience," and the guy at the office supply store said he didn't have the "aptitude" to work there. Keith didn't even know what that fancy word meant.

He shuffled from place to place being told he wasn't qualified or that the opening had been filled. He had gone two-thirds of the way through the horseshoe when he came upon *Fletcher's* scripted in white lettering on a red sign. The name of the place was above the phone number and to the other side was printed in bold letters, *Pizza-Subs-Chicken.* As he trudged through the door, his brow dripped with sweat and his legs wobbled.

A red-haired waitress looked up from wiping a table and growled, "What do you want?"

"I saw a *Help Wanted* sign outside," said Keith. "I want to apply for a job."

"Mr. Fletcher, are we still hiring?" she asked.

A man behind the counter, who had black hair slicked back with gel and chubby cheeks covered with 5 o'clock shadow, replied, "Give him an application."

The waitress came back with a form and a short pencil. "Fill this out."

Keith sat at a table and put down his name, social security number, and not much else. He saw customers flowing into and out of *Fletcher's*. He didn't know what the owner would think when he looked at the form, which was almost blank.

The waitress came back and picked it up. She huffed, "Mr. Fletcher."

The middle-aged man, who had a large beer-belly bulging underneath a white apron, waddled forth from behind the counter. He scanned the application and said, "I've watched you walk the length of the mall. You got drive. But you're not the only wise guy in the world. I was young once. It says you're only fifteen?"

"That's right," said Keith, wondering if he was old enough to get a job.

"Your mother or father must fill out this work permit and sign it." The man handed Keith a preprinted form with the employer information already filled in.

"Sure, my mom can do that."

"One more thing," said Mr. Fletcher. "Go down to the barbershop tomorrow morning and get a haircut. You start at eleven."

"Yes, sir," blurted out Keith. He left the shop all jittery, but hopeful. This would be his first job.

When Keith moseyed into the barber shop the next morning, a couple men were already sitting there reading sports magazines and chatting about the Ravens offensive shortcomings. Even so the barber barked out, "Young man, it's your turn."

Keith nestled into the highchair and mumbled, "Trim my hair."

The barber fastened a yellow bib around his neck and remarked, "Mr. Fletcher said to expect you this morning. He told me how to cut your hair." He lopped off his locks in back and used an electric trimmer to shorn his hair close on both sides.

Keith felt like he had joined the military, but what choice did he have? He couldn't weasel out of paying that damn dinner bill.

Keith entered the sub shop a few minutes before 11 a.m. He saw Mr. Fletcher with a grim look on his face. He hoped that his boss hadn't made a mistake and hired too many employees. He didn't want to be fired before he even started.

"Wilkins told me about you," stated Mr. Fletcher. "He said you've been snooping around the new townhouses."

"Who's Wilkins?" asked Keith.

"Officer Wilkins," said Joyce, the red-haired waitress. She pursed her lips and squinted at him as though he was a bug that should be squashed.

Keith realized he had already made an enemy.

"We'll give you a chance," said Mr. Fletcher. "Any funny business …and you go." He stood up and called out, "Lenny, show him where the dishrags and racks are."

"Yes, sir."

Lenny, an older boy with peach fuzz on his chin, showed Keith how to bus the tables by collecting the plastic mugs and ceramic plates used to give customers an upscale dining experience. Then they wiped the tabletops clean of spilled sodas and spots of tomato sauce that had dripped off of pizza slices and sometimes picked up chicken bones left scattered on the floor. Lenny also showed him how to rack the dishes and wash the pots and pans by hand.

Meanwhile, Keith observed Joyce ringing up customers and slipping the big bills, including a $50 one, under the cash register tray. The biggest bill he had ever seen before was a $20 his mother gave him on his birthday. The rest of the year he wished he had an allowance like the other kids in school. He hoped that when Joyce wasn't looking his sticky fingers could pocket a couple $50 bills. That would go a long way to paying off his debt.

Lenny and Keith worked together during lunch to clear the tables and wash all the dishes. Around 3 p.m. they were done. Lenny went outside to smoke a cigarette while Keith lounged at a table.

"What are you doing?" snapped Mr. Fletcher.

Keith looked up at his boss, his mouth hanging open in shock. He didn't know he wasn't allowed to take a break yet.

"Go in the back with Joyce," ordered Mr. Fletcher. "She'll show you which boxes to bring out. It's that time of year, you know."

Keith lugged out four boxes covered with dust from the stockroom, smearing his clothes and making him wheeze. Upon opening them, he found a bunch of Christmas lights and other ornaments wrapped in old newspapers. He sat on the floor, trying to untangle the string of lights. His mother would never spend money on something this extravagant. Her paycheck went toward buying food and electricity for their apartment. He couldn't understand how putting up a bunch of dumb decorations could change how people thought or behaved. He wondered what Mr. Fletcher's angle was. Perhaps if customers were snookered into believing this stuff, they would stay longer and spend more money. It would make the bling of the cash register ring out throughout the shop more often.

"Stop playing with those lights," sneered Joyce. "We only got two hours to put them up."

"I'm getting there," said Keith.

Just then the door swung open and a mechanic from the gas station down the street shuffled in with his gray uniform being spotted with grease.

"Bob, you're late today," gushed Joyce.

"I was putting a muffler on an old Ford."

"Mr. Fletcher," she called out, "a cheeseburger sub, hold the mayo, and fries on the crisp side."

"How do you remember?" asked Bob.

Joyce smirked and said, "We take care of our regulars."

The mechanic trudged over to a table and plopped down, sticking his shoes into the aisle. He leaned back in the chair and sighed.

Joyce plunked a roll of masking tape near Keith and grunted, "Tape the lights in place." She had plenty of joy for the customers, but none reserved for him.

Keith spent almost an hour taping the lights around the inside edge of the window. Joyce fastened silver tinsel along the length of the counter and hung a mistletoe near the *Pick-up Order* station. A middle-aged woman and two preteen kids came into the restaurant and plopped down at a table of their own.

Mr. Fletcher stood underneath the mistletoe and called out, "Hey, beautiful, come over here."

The woman, who had a pudgy figure, stepped across from him.

Mr. Fletcher shook his stomach and swung his arms as though doing an old-fashioned dance called The Twist, which Keith recalled seeing in a grainy black-and-white video shown on television. Mr. Fletcher groaned, "Oh, baby."

The woman squealed, "Oh, Johnny."

Mr. Fletcher hugged her, and they smooched loud enough for everyone to hear.

When they broke apart, she hollered, "My man's still got it."

"I'll see you later," quipped Mr. Fletcher.

His wife grinned and left with their two children in tow.

More customers trickled in. Keith pretended to wipe the counter, inching closer to the cash register. Occasionally, Joyce bent over to grab napkins or straws from underneath. When she did, she took her eyes off the tray. Maybe if he got close enough, he could swipe a $50 bill without her knowing it. Now he was only a foot away. Joyce smiled at a customer and asked "How was your meal?"

"Fine," replied the man, who paid with a credit card.

Then she spun toward Keith and snapped, "Get all the corners. That's where the dirt is."

"Okay," he muttered, working his rag around the edges. Every time he got near her, the joy disappeared from her face and voice. He went back to the dishwashing machine and leaned against its steel frame. How could he get close enough to the cash register to get a holiday bonus? While he poured over the possible scenarios in his mind, Officer Wilkins marched into the restaurant. Keith hunkered down to washing the dishes so the policeman wouldn't notice him.

The officer spoke to Mr. Fletcher, "John, you and George at the auto parts store are thinking the same thing. Both of you are putting up your decorations."

"People are happy around Christmas," stated Mr. Fletcher. "It's time to forget grudges and love everyone again."

"That may be true for you," said Officer Wilkins, "but the criminals go where the cash is. Unfortunately, I'll be busy."

They continued chatting about something when Keith heard a lady nearby ask, "Don't you see where we are?"

Her boyfriend looked around and replied, "In a sub shop."

She tilted her head and gazed above.

Then he spotted the mistletoe. "Oh!"

Their lips smacked, and the woman purred with delight.

Keith was surprised that some doodad hanging from the ceiling could make women act so goofy. He couldn't imagine working here on Saturday night when the older guys in his high school brought in their sweethearts for a special dinner. It would be unbearable.

The following Tuesday Keith hurried home from school, crunched his homework, getting a slight migraine from solving algebra problems, and bolted out the door. He ate a snack while sprinting toward *Fletcher's* in the shopping center. He had to be on time. He hustled into the sub shop wheezing to catch his breath.

"You came back!" Joyce snickered. "Mr. Fletcher, look what the wind blew in."

There was still no joy in her voice. His boss was hunched over the grill, frying a steak for a customer's sub. The odor of simmering onions wafted through the air.

Keith fastened a dishwasher apron around his waist and bussed the tables. Then he racked the plastic mugs and ceramic plates and pushed the rack into the machine. The whoosh-wash of the machine sounded soothing compared to Joyce's screeching.

He heard Joyce barking, "The new waitress, Colby, is here."

Keith glanced over there and saw a teenage girl, wearing a soiled blouse and slacks, who looked like a tomboy with her blonde hair twilled into a bird's nest, hollow cheeks, and flat chest.

"Take her into the back and comb her hair," ordered Mr. Fletcher.

Joyce disappeared with the girl.

Fifteen minutes later they emerged from the Ladies Room. Colby had her blonde hair fluffed over her forehead and ears, and a touch of makeup on her face. Keith thought she looked like an adorable doll.

"Is that what you wear on the first day of a new job?" scoffed Joyce.

"I don't always dress like this," stated Colby. She tilted her chin up and looked away. Then she peered right at her and said, "Last spring my mother bought me a chiffon dress for my junior prom that cost $800. She's always buying me dresses and pocketbooks. I got pocketbooks made by designers from all over the world. Today I'm dressing down in case I spill food on my clothes. And I can't bring my pocketbooks in here because I might lose them."

"You still have to look like a waitress," said Joyce. "We'll put you in a full apron. We were saving these for the week before Christmas, but you can wear one early." She gave her a bright green apron.

Colby wrapped it around herself and whined, "It doesn't go with my hair."

"You're supposed to be an elf," stated Joyce. "Elves grin because they're happy and they work hard."

"Right," she grunted. Colby picked up a tray and trudged to a table. She put the plates in front of the patrons without saying a word. Then she plodded back.

"I guess you don't have a dad to buy you stuff," said Keith. "I live with my mom too."

"My father is a heart surgeon," huffed Colby. She tilted her chin up and gazed away for a moment. Then she stared at him and said, "He's working in the Philippines teaching them how to transplant hearts."

Keith looked outside at all the old cars in the parking lot and going by in the street. He asked, "Why are you living in this neighborhood?"

Colby looked away and then said, "He gave his last yearly paycheck to the people in Liberia to help them with the Ebola crisis."

"If that is what you want me to believe…okay."

Colby went about serving customers. Sometimes she took their orders and returned with their sodas and shakes, letting Joyce bring out their subs and pizza. Other times she brought their entrees right to the table. The women put their tips in a jar by the cash register, which slowly filled up. Even so Keith could tell that Colby hadn't warmed up to the work.

When she came back with an empty tray, he asked, "How did you end up here?"

"I was throwing rocks at the school," she replied, "and accidentally broke a couple windows. A policeman caught me. He said if I didn't tell him who I was, he would bust me. I told him he can't arrest a woman."

"What happened?"

"He did. Now I've got to pay $300 for the windows and $125 court costs. How about you?"

"Some jerk said I was a peeping Tom," sneered Keith. "He said I ruined his wife's birthday. So he went out on the town and bought her a really *nice* dinner. Now I got to pay him back $516."

"Wow!" she gasped, raising her eyebrows. "I thought I had to pay a lot… Are you?"

"Am I what?"

"A peeping Tom?"

"Don't be ridiculous," he scoffed. "I wanted to see how other people lived. Now I'll be working here forever."

She sighed, "Forever is a long time."

"I don't understand why Mr. Fletcher hired us," said Keith.

"Some people are just dumb."

A lot of people stopped in the sub shop after 5 p.m. to pick up orders to take home for dinner or to grab a bite to eat. Colby rushed about and waited on the tables. Keith swooped in about 20 minutes later to bus them. Once in a while he watched her work, her slender arms placing the plates and cups in front of the customers and her tush wagging down the aisle. Not once did he think about getting sticky fingers even though he passed by the cash register quite often. A little after 6 p.m. Mr. Fletcher said, "Colby and Keith, why don't you take a break? Sit at the booth by the window."

Keith got a Pepsi and Colby poured herself an orange drink. When they sat across from each other in the booth, the fading sunshine fell across their faces, highlighting Colby's elegant neck and chin. Keith said, "You look pretty with the sun shining off your hair."

"Sure," she smirked. "I probably look like a giant grasshopper."

"No. I like the way…"

She loosened her apron and folded the top in her lap, revealing her tattered blue blouse which made her prettier to him.

"…you look. You're hot."

They slurped their sodas, glancing at each other. He gathered his nerve and said, "There's some mistletoe hanging over there. When you stand underneath it, you are supposed to kiss the person you're with."

Colby looked at the mistletoe and tilted her chin up. Then she gazed straight at him and said, "I used to have a boyfriend from Texas who wore a Stetson hat and cowboy boots. He had to wear the boots because you need them when you round up steers. His kisses were really big. Once he gave me a kiss that lasted…ten minutes."

"Really?" gasped Keith. "Oh, wow!"

"And I had another boyfriend who was a desperado with a gang. He rode a motorcycle and wore a black leather jacket. He was always looking over his shoulder for the police. He wouldn't come to the front of my house. So he kissed me on the back porch."

"That's amazing."

"It really was."

"So…what's it like being kissed?"

Colby squirmed in her chair. "What's it like?"

Keith leaned forward. "Yeah, what's it like?"

"Well…ah…" Her shoulders twitched and she looked all over the place, everywhere except at him. Then her lip quivered and she looked at him in a perplexed way.

"You never been kissed before either?"

She muttered, "No."

"I guess we could go over there," he suggested. "It's on the way back behind the counter."

"Or we could end our breaks at separate times."

"Or at the same time."

A wisp of a smile appeared on her lips.

He got up. She did the same. They walked apart, but toward the back of the restaurant. When they got near the mistletoe, they stepped toward each other. He peeked above. She did too.

Its oval leaves shimmered lime-green and berries gleamed pearl-white. The aura of spring hung above them though the air outside was frigid and snow clung to the ground.

Keith was unsure of where to put his hands. Should he hug her? Their faces were only inches apart.

Her pink lips were as beautiful as coral.

He leaned closer and their lips touched. In that moment it seemed like all the clocks in the world had stopped and even the beating of his own heart. The kiss came naturally. It was the most fantastic thing in the world. When they stepped back, he peered into her eyes, which were as blue as sapphires.

She giggled. Then she galloped behind the counter with her face shining.

He plodded back there pretending that nothing had happened. But for a brief moment the magic of Christmas fell upon them.

Hatred Isn't a Word

That is strong enough to describe how the guys feel about Rodney. Despised and loathed are a better description because he has ruined every family gathering at Christmas by bringing that long red stocking. They're supposed to be ornamental. People hang them over their fake fireplaces and reminisce about how ages ago folks cooked and heated their homes by burning logs. Rodney just doesn't get it. Last year he gave my wife a Martha Stewart cookbook and said, "Wanda, you are one of the best cooks I know. I figure the two of you are at the same level of culinary artistry."

She smiled while skimming through the pages and her misty blue eyes glistened. Then a severe look gripped her face as she grumbled, "Kurt never compliments me on my meals or helps in the kitchen. But Rodney," and she grinned again, "compares me to a master chef."

All the other wives began harping about their husbands. It continued into the wee hours of the morning until all the eggnog was drained.

I don't know what Rodney is going to do this year to turn the tide in his favor and against us. I hope he doesn't show up.

I start to implement my secret plan to draw attention away from him even before he gets here. At 9 a.m. my son, Edwin, who's still a boy with chubby cheeks and good manners, is eager to open his Christmas presents. The one I brought him is wrapped in bright silver paper and larger than a microwave. Tearing off the wrapping, he gasps, "Oh, wow!"

On the side of the box is a photo of an UAV, unmanned aerial vehicle. It is shaped like an X with two wings and four propellers, two on each wing.

"Let's go outside and start it up," I suggest.

"Cool," he replies.

"Kurt, do you think he's old enough for a present like that?" asks Wanda, who is shaking her head of honey-blond hair.

"Sure," I say. "He'll be moving on to middle school in a couple years."

We grab our coats from the closet and carry the box through the kitchen, which is filled with the smell of a freshly baked apple strudel. We step into the backyard and set the box down. Our beagle pokes his snout out the door, but retreats inside because of the frigid temperature. Outside every tree's gnarled limbs are bare and wispy gray clouds block out the sun. Even so visibility is clear so we unpack the drone. Setting it up, we see a marvel of engineering from its white hull to the four bright-orange propeller blades.

I roar, "Start the engine!"

"Dad, I don't know how," replies my son, inspecting the control box.

I crouch down and look at all the levers and throttle. I'm not too sure what to do either. "Give me a minute." I slip on my reading glasses and break out the instruction manual which is 62 pages long. Flipping through several pages, I find the starting sequence. I set the controls and push the green button.

The propeller blades whirl and the drone lifts up into the air, but hovers in a stationary position. I yank the throttle every which way, but the drone won't move. I bring it back down to the ground and tell Edwin, "Why don't you try it until I figure out how to change directions."

My son plays with the drone, making the engine hum and watching it take off and land. He operates the aircraft until he gets tired. I'm on page 23, but still can't figure out how to fly this thing.

"Dad," he says, "it's getting cold out here."

"I'm chilly too," I admit. "Let's go inside and warm up. We'll come back out later.'"

We scoot into the kitchen and grab cups of hot chocolate. Hearing voices coming from the living room, I scurry in there and greet Gretchen, my sister, and Drew, her husband. My sister is outfitted in a traditional dress, making her look like a Bavarian beer maiden, while her husband's knit shirt shows off his stocky beer-drinking build.

A car chugs down the street and its muffler backfires. Rodney calls them vintage automobiles, but I see them for the junk heaps they are. The chugging stops right outside our home.

Edwin rushes into the living room and yelps, "It's Uncle Rodney."

"Not so fast," I say. "Go back and finish your hot chocolate."

My son wheels around and trudges into the kitchen.

I pull back the window curtain and see Rodney's junk heap, which has a green box-shaped body and a black top. He lumbers up the sidewalk dragging that damn red stocking. Rodney is a thin man because he has to stand up all day long working in an auto parts store while I couldn't lose the bulge around my waist if a doctor put me on a crash diet for a month. He rings the bell, then raps with his knuckles.

My wife opens the door, saying, "Rodney, come on in. We're glad to see you."

He is wearing a sport coat over his white shirt and shiny black shoes that stick out from his denim jeans. He grips the red stocking in his hands. Placing it by the door, the stocking stands up by itself because it's so full of gifts. It is three feet tall and trimmed with white wool at the top. Rodney must think that Santa is a giant.

"We heard you coming up the road," I scoff.

"What type of car is that?" asks my wife as though she's curious.

"A '78 Dodge Charger with a B-body," states Rodney. "I'm going to fix it up and resell it to a customer. All those classic cars hug the road and have that growl."

"It sounds like a hole in the muffler to me," quips Drew, my brother-in-law, who is still sitting on the sofa.

Kapow! He clobbered Rodney as soon as he stepped into the house. I high-five his raised hand.

"Is Edwin here?" asks Rodney, shaking off the jab. "My first gift is for him."

"My boy's in the kitchen." I follow him down the hallway into the warm kitchen.

Edwin looks up from his cup of hot chocolate.

"I understand that you and Floppy haven't been getting along lately," says Rodney.

"He's getting old, I guess," replies Edwin.

"That's why I got a gift for both of you."

"Both of us?"

Rodney takes a box the size of my fist out of the stocking. I notice that grease is stuck underneath his fingernails from tinkering with car engines. He hands the gift to my son.

Edwin peels off the wrapping paper and opens the box to reveal a yellow ball with something scribbled on it in black magic marker.

"It's a Floppy Ball," states Rodney. "Bounce it up and down and see what happens."

My son bounces the ball.

Our beagle, Floppy, runs into the kitchen.

"Keep doing it," says Rodney.

Floppy jumps up and down with the rhythm of the ball. A low-pitched growl comes from the dog's throat and a couple high-pitched barks.

"Now go downstairs and play with him."

"Cool." My son scampers downstairs into the basement with the beagle right behind him. He screams, "Thanks, Uncle Rodney."

"I don't understand," I say. "He's got a new gift right outside. And it cost me a fortune."

"Maybe you don't understand your boy," says Rodney.

"That's just a tennis ball with the word, Floppy, written on it."

"If it brings him fun what difference does it make?" says Rodney, grinning with satisfaction.

"Difference? That's my son!"

Wanda plods into the kitchen and pulls open the oven door. She bastes the turkey, which gives off a roasting odor.

"I got a gift for you too, Wanda."

"For me?" She unwraps a package to reveal a funky color of yarn in-between orange and red.

"It's vermillion," says Rodney.

She shakes her head in disbelief and says, "I've been looking for that shade for months. Thanks for taking an interest in my crocheting." She glances at me. "Sometimes adults should give something else besides gift cards to each other."

"But you go to that store," I protest.

"It's just like when I find a part for a customer," states Rodney. "They think they need sparkplugs, but actually need an engine flush. A bottle of cleaner does the trick."

"You have a special place in my heart," says Wanda.

"I got a gift for Gretchen," he says, skipping into the living room.

"I can't stand that guy," I seethe.

"Kurt!" gasps my wife. "How can you say that about your brother?"

"I got to read this instruction manual," I mumble. I find a section about using algorithms to chart a flight path on a map and scan the diagrams, but decide to postpone serious study until tomorrow. Today I got to keep an eye on my brother.

My wife opens the oven and bastes the turkey again. Her nimble fingers cut up carrots, shell peas, and pour a cup of water in a pot. Then she simmers gravy in a pan to go with the meal.

Rodney comes back into the kitchen and hands me a thin package from the red stocking. "Kurt, I almost forgot. Here's a present for you."

I look at the cheerful wrapping on the outside and cringe. Now I'll have to pretend I like his gift.

"Go ahead," says Rodney. "Open it."

I tear off the wrapping and lift the lid off the box. It is a tie he probably bought in a bargain bin at a department store.

"That will go with your brown suit," says Wanda. "What do you want to say to your brother?"

I hiss, "Thanks."

"I've got to find Drew," says Rodney, turning around. He skips back into the living room.

"What did you get for your brother?" mocks my wife.

"I go down to his store all the time to buy parts for our cars," I reply. "Where do you think I got your windshield wipers last month?"

"That's not a gift," scoffs Wanda.

"People like me are giving him a job."

"Oh, Kurt!" she yelps.

I watch her checking the pots and pans on the stove and in the oven. A moment later she bounds into the living room. I get up and follow her. I don't want to be a snoop, but you never know what Rodney is up to.

Stepping into the living room, I see him nestled on the chair next to the front door. Gretchen, my sister, is admiring a scarf that he got for her. Her husband, Drew, has trotted off to the family room to watch a basketball game on television.

The doorbell rings twice. When Wanda opens the front door, she says, "Loretta, it's good you could show up."

"I was held up by traffic," she says.

My wife grabs her coat and hangs it up in the closet.

Meanwhile, Rodney leers at her like a kid looking at an ice cream cone.

Even though I love my wife, I must admit that Loretta has a pretty face with a button nose and wide lips. Her shoulder-length brunette hair used to be combed straight. It's still parted in the middle, but now wavy from her hazel eyes to her shoulders, making her look like a country girl though she has never lived on a farm. Whenever she comes near, the faint smell of violets linger. Her dresses used to be plain, but now have shorter hems above the knee and more frills and lace. This one has a low neckline and is sky-blue.

Rodney combs his short brown hair with his fingers and steps closer. He kisses her and says, "Your lips taste like sangria."

"Oh, honey," says Loretta. They go off in the corner and whisper to each other.

"It's so romantic," gushes Wanda.

I sneer, "He's quoting a line from a Blake Sheldon song."

"You never do it," snaps my wife.

"Well, I'm your husband."

"Yes, you are," she says like it's a bad thing. She storms back into the kitchen.

First, it was my son. Now Rodney is turning my wife against me.

Rodney sits on the sofa and chats with Loretta, who works with my wife. He met her at a 4th of July gathering several years ago, and she has been hanging around ever since. The last time I saw them together was on Labor Day. They talked about how they went line dancing together and both liked barbecued food. If the music doesn't feature a fiddle, then they don't listen. So I put on a CD of old-fashioned jazz ballads with cymbals clashing and a saxophone wailing. Maybe that will upset them and they'll leave. At least I can't see that smart-aleck too clearly since the only light in the dim living room is coming from an advent wreath, with four lit candles, set on the coffee table.

Instead I see the silhouette of their heads bobbing to the rhythm. Then they start smooching again. Wanda returns from another round of turkey basting and sits next to me.

"The last couple gifts are for Loretta," blares Rodney.

Loretta reaches into the red stocking up to her elbow and retrieves a rectangular box. When she unwraps it, he leans closer to see her reaction. "Rodney?" she gasps, gazing around the room.

"You said you were having trouble finding them."

"What is it?" asks Gretchen.

"A pair of silk stockings," reveals Loretta.

"I don't think this is the place for that type of gift," says Wanda. "We have a child in the house."

"Any man can go to a lingerie shop," scoffs Gretchen.

"There's one more gift in the stocking," says Rodney.

The women keep carping about the lousy gift Rodney has given his girlfriend. I walk into the family room where Drew is watching the Knicks and Spurs galloping up and down the court. The sound of squeaking sneakers is coming from the television while from the living room I hear my brother getting pecked to death by a flock of hens. I gloat, "It looks like Rodney is finally getting his."

"You can only fool them for so long," comments Drew.

"Hey, I like your Knicks cap," I say, trying to change the subject. "Did you get that on the internet?"

Drew rolls his eyes and motions with a flick of his head back to the living room. No matter what we do we can't get away from my pesky brother.

We watch the Knicks go on a scoring spree with Carmelo Anthony roaring down the lane to put in layups and swatting away shots on the defensive end to create fast breaks. It is getting close to halftime when Wanda pokes her head into the room and asks, "Are you guys ready for dinner?"

"Yeah…Sure," we reply.

Walking into the living room, I notice that all the women are quiet. "What happened?" I ask. "Did Rodney go home?"

"Look what he gave me," says Loretta, holding out her left hand. "He said I was the most beautiful woman he ever met."

I look at the ring, which holds only a speck of a diamond. The one I bought for my wife was three times bigger. Then I look at her pudgy figure and shake my head.

"It was so sweet seeing him get down on one knee and propose," says Gretchen. "He's in the kitchen helping your wife."

I hurry in there and grab a bowl of sauerkraut. Carrying it into the dining room, I see Rodney setting the serving plate with the roasted turkey in the table's center. The women bring in bowls of peas & carrots, kale, stuffing seasoned with sausage, cranberries, and potato dumplings. Everyone sits down at the table. Steam shimmers off the food.

"Rodney, take off your coat," says Wanda. "It's hot in here."

"No, I really don't want to."

His fiancée gets up and slips it off for him, saying, "Come on. Don't be a baby."

Everyone sees his worn dress shirt. The collar has holes, a rip near the pocket has been stitched together, and a couple of buttons have popped off, giving a glimpse of his white T-shirt.

I see my chance to put him in his place by saying, "No wonder they make you wear a uniform at work."

"I've seen scarecrows better dressed than that," chimes in Drew.

Rodney blushes from embarrassment and says, "I haven't been able to buy a new one because I was saving up money for the ring and all." He stares down in shame.

"Aw!" gushes my wife. "I think it's sweet. He gave the shirt off his back for Loretta." She glares at me and declares, "My husband had to go to Miami Beach on spring vacation with his buddies before he proposed to me."

"I went there with my fraternity," I explain. "What's wrong with that?"

Wanda looks away. She always does that when she doesn't like what I say.

"I had to wait an extra year," huffs Gretchen, "because Drew bought a Camaro."

Drew grunts. He squints at Rodney, and then teases Loretta, "Tell us how you feel about his shirt."

"I'm happy he wants me to be his shotgun rider," says Loretta, perking up in her seat. She turns her head and peers at her beau with seductive eyes.

The couple gaze at each other while the food is getting cold. Even our beagle has enough sense to chow down before laying in the corner to daydream.

"That's a lovely shirt, Rodney," says Wanda, getting up from the table. She comes around and stands behind him. "Let me help you put this bib on. We don't want you to spill any gravy on it."

"Would you like some stuffing, Rodney?" asks Gretchen, leaning over the table and holding a serving spoon.

All the women are going gaga over him while he is grinning again. Even my son looks amazed when he peers at him.

I'm breathing hard and Drew is gritting his teeth. Like I said, Hatred isn't a word that is strong enough.

Tie a Yellow Ribbon...

Ruth had trouble making ends meet because she was a single mom and the child support was slow in coming in. When she got home after a long day at work, she would flop on the sofa and watch the evening news while her daughter, Melissa, did her homework. Ruth was dismayed as she heard a national news anchor apologize for telling a fib: The helicopter his news team traveled in while reporting from Iraq was not forced down after being hit by an R.P.G. (rocket-propelled grenade). The newsman was subsequently suspended for six months from his network. The same year a Hollywood celebrity was tried on social media and found guilty of committing a felony without benefit of a judge or jury. Now protestors appeared at every venue where he performed and carried placards condemning his supposed crime. State governments also got involved in political correctness by rushing to remove confederate symbols from their cities and towns in an attempt to erase history. And a local school teacher was fired from her job teaching students in the 7th grade because she posted a photo of herself drinking a glass of wine at a French chateau while on vacation in Europe. Parents created a firestorm of protest and demanded that this "drunk" not be allowed to negatively influence their children in the classroom. Ruth hoped that her daughter would never have to endure the consequences of making a mistake. Melissa was only nine years old and still lived inside a fantasy bubble. Unfortunately, Ruth didn't realize that her daughter's politically incorrect actions were about to bring the weight of the world to bear.

Nothing would have happened had it not been for a busted water pipe. Some unknown delinquent broke a window in her daughter's school, letting in the frigid night air which froze everything inside the building's basement. So on Monday morning there was no running water for the students. Ruth took her daughter to work with her. She pulled Melissa's long brown hair into a pony tail and placed a mask over her mouth and nose, worried that her daughter could pass germs to the patients or pick up an infection from them. When they entered the ward, a patient called out, "Whoa, what's this? We got a big one and little one. Missy, are you going to be a nurse?"

"Uh-huh," said the little one.

"This is my daughter, Melissa," said Ruth. "Let's not have any rough talk today."

"Yes, ma'am," said the man.

There were a half dozen soldiers in D ward. The ones who sat up in their beds or moved about had short hair on the sides, but the one who was bedridden had longer, untrimmed hair. Ruth went to the nearest bed and asked, "How are you doing today, Sergeant Knox?"

"I'm up," he replied. "I hope to be moving around in a day or two."

Ruth wrapped a cuff around his arm to take his blood pressure. "I want you to get better so you can do P.T. (physical therapy)."

The bed sheet was indented from the stump that was left on the man's leg. Ruth peeked at Melissa, who probably realized he had been hurt somewhere, but was still innocent about war and peace.

"I could get better real soon if you promise to go dancing with me," quipped the sergeant.

"My job is to get you well," said Ruth.

"Come on, Sarge," said a soldier, who was also missing a leg, and was scooting around in a wheelchair. He stopped and spun around to face them. "You might get some fast wheels like me."

They strolled to a bed on the other side of the room. A large man with a square chin greeted them. His arms had bulging biceps, but his legs consisted of two stumps. He said, "I don't know what you're complaining about, Sarge. Us black folks always got to do twice as much as you white folks." Then he said to Ruth, "I'm going to get so good at moving about that I'll be running the Boston Marathon two years from now. This Motown man will learn how to fly."

"Is that so?" asked Ruth.

"You can count on it as the sun rises."

The soldier in the wheelchair rolled forward and stopped in front of them. Ruth said, "Private Epstein, I guess you want to be next?"

"Let's get it over with," he replied. "In a moment I'll be hot-rodding down the hallway just like a song from the Boss, *Born to Run*."

Ruth recorded his temperature and blood pressure. She took a vial of blood while he was propped up in the wheelchair. She labeled the tube and placed it in a mechanical contraption by the door. After she punched in the lab's location, the three-foot robot lit up and spun around. It rolled down the hallway with a whining sound.

A Marine in a blue dress uniform, decorated with a row of ribbons on his left chest, and an elderly man in a gray suit had entered the ward. They stood next to the bedridden soldier, who was missing both an arm and a leg. The man in the gray suit said something and the Marine pinned a medal on the nightstand next to the bed. "Private Chavez," said the officer loud enough for everyone to hear. They both saluted him.

The soldier, who was lying on his back, brought his remaining hand up to his temple and saluted back.

The men turned and marched out of the ward. Private Epstein rolled over in his wheelchair and asked, "What did those fuddy-duddies give you?"

The man in the next bed turned onto his side and said, "It's a purple heart."

"I'd rather have a yellow ribbon," admitted Chavez.

"A yellow ribbon?" asked Private Epstein. "Were you afraid of combat?"

"My wife, Isabel, says she tied yellow ribbons around the mesquite bush in front of our home," said Chavez. "I can't wait to fly home to Austin to see them."

"You should Skype her," suggested Private Epstein.

"He has to get better before they let him do that," said Sergeant Knox. "He looks like Casper the ghost."

Chavez got a tired look on his face. "Whatever." He dozed off.

"That boy must have done something special," said the black vet.

The ward became quiet as the soldiers contemplated the deed he must have done.

When Melissa and her mom went over there, Chavez was out cold. Ruth took the man's readings and jotted them down on his medical chart.

Melissa looked at the medal fastened to the end of the purple ribbon. It had a golden profile of George Washington enclosed by a purple heart, which was gilded in gold. She asked, "How can they be so brave?"

"We're Marines," said Sergeant Knox. "Whether it's on the battlefield or off, we are too stubborn to be scared and have too much work to do to be sad."

The next day Ruth was glad that Dora, Melissa's best friend from the local Girl Scout troop, came to their home carrying craft paper. Dora's complexion was as dark as black coffee and her personality as sweet as sugar. Dora always challenged Melissa with new shapes and patterns whenever they did art projects together. Ruth was sure the same thing would happen today. Melissa drew an outline of a snowman with a black magic marker on the cover of a card, affixed buttons for its eyes, sewed on a scrap of twill cloth for its scarf, and attached cotton swabs for its arms. She scrawled part of the slogan "Frosty wishes…" on the cover and finished it inside the card, "…you a happy holiday to warm your heart." Inside she drew several stuffed stockings hanging over a fireplace with flames curling around logs and a window looking out to the snowman. Meanwhile, Dora created a colorful card of her own with a patriotic theme. They fashioned other cards using different colored paper for the base, pencil and magic markers for the outlines of objects, sprinkled glitter on glue to make sunshine or star shine, and used items found in a sewing kit to finish them. Ruth could tell that they had done a good job, but didn't know that several cards would not pass the hospital's censor.

On Wednesday afternoon Ruth brought her daughter back to D Ward. The soldiers had a visiting hour, but only relatives of Private Epstein, who lived in New Jersey and could drive there, would show up. Ruth thought the cards would cheer up the wounded soldiers. Their faces brightened when they opened the envelopes and saw what was within.

"Does this beat all?" said Sergeant Knox. On his card the phrase "Merry Christmas" was written overtop an American flag drawn with red and white stripes as bright as a candy cane and white stars blazing on a blue background.

"Hey, you got a black Santa Claus on here," shouted the African-American soldier in amazement. He turned his card so everyone could see the picture of Santa in a red suit and cap with a bushy-white beard and skin as brown as chocolate. "How did you know I wanted to see a black Santa?"

"My friend, Dora, helped me make that," said Melissa.

"You should have more friends like her."

Melissa handed the next card to Private Epstein.

He had a perplexed look as he pulled it from the envelope. Then a grin sprouted forth. "This is sweet," he said. "You got a blue Star of David, wooden dreidel, and menorah sitting on a windowsill. This must be..."

"A Hanukkah house," said Melissa. "It looks like the one in our neighborhood."

Finally, Melissa gave the last card to Private Chavez. It featured a drawing of a mesquite bush on the front, but a real yellow ribbon pinned to it.

The soldier's eyes welled up. He stammered, "This reminds me of home."

"I remember that Tony Orlando song," said the sergeant. "It was about a sweetheart waiting for her man to come home."

"And if there wasn't a yellow ribbon tied around a tree," said Private Epstein, "he would stay on the bus and forget about her. But I can't remember how it goes."

Another soldier hummed the tune.

"I remember some of it," said Ruth. She started to sing the song:

I'm coming home, I've done my time.
Now I've got to know what is and isn't mine.
If you received my letter telling you I'd soon be free
Then you'll know just what to do.
If you still want me, if you still want me

Tie a yellow ribbon 'round the ole oak tree.
It's been three long years, do you still want me?

Her voice was not mellifluous, but reedy. Melissa often heard her in church singing hymns, but this was the first time she sang a song heard on the radio.

Bus driver, please look for me
'Cause I couldn't bear to see…

A woman's voice bellowed, drowning out Ruth's singing, "What's going on?"

Ruth's mouth hung open while everyone looked in the opposite direction.

A stout woman, who appeared agitated as though a girdle was pinching her hips too tight, had entered the ward. She scanned the room, noting all the cards on the bedside tables. Then she thumbed through a booklet of authorized carols, saying, "That's not *Jingle Bells* or *Winter Wonderland*."

"It's *Tie a Yellow Ribbon Round the Ole Oak Tree*," recalled Ruth.

"You're singing an unauthorized carol?"

The sergeant quipped, "It's a pop song, Ms. Bludgeon."

"Huh!?" Ms. Bludgeon leaned against the wall, applying all her weight to the pushing of the intercom button. She screamed, "Code Red in D Ward. Code Red in D Ward."

A moment later two MPs barged into the ward. One had his gun drawn. The other had a Taser ready. Their eyes were ice-cold and their fingers were itching to pull the trigger.

"Confiscate all these cards," ordered Ms. Bludgeon. "They are contraband."

The MPs grabbed an empty plastic trash can and plodded around the room, placing the cards inside.

"I'm sorry, Ms. Bludgeon," said Ruth, who wondered if her boss ever had a childhood.

"You have intentionally violated the rules spelled out in the employee handbook. Religious displays are prohibited inside this hospital."

"We were just trying to…"

"Follow us to the administrator's office," stated Ms. Bludgeon.

"Ms. Bludgeon, you don't have to act like that," said Sergeant Knox. "I've got you second on my dance card."

Ms. Bludgeon huffed, "This way."

Some soldiers laughed and others winced because another C.O. (commanding officer) had come down on them. Then D Ward became as still and quiet as a cemetery.

Ms. Bludgeon walked stiffly behind the MP who carried the plastic trash can. Ruth was worried. Melissa wasn't old enough to understand the trouble she had gotten her into. Ms. Bludgeon barged into the administrator's office and asked, "Where is Ms. Timmons?"

"She's at a conference in Washington, D.C. this afternoon," responded her assistant. "She'll be back tomorrow morning."

"Send her a message," shouted Ms. Bludgeon. "I must discuss a disciplinary matter with her at 9 a.m. sharp."

"Yes, Ms. Bludgeon," said the assistant, whose hand trembled.

The next morning a half dozen picketers marched in a solemn procession back and forth in front of the hospital's main entrance, making Ruth wondered whether a group of employees was striking over working conditions. She could hear the dreary plodding of their boots the closer she got. Then she saw signs that shocked her. A middle-aged woman wrapped in a long black coat carried one that announced, "God is dead." An older man with a crew cut toted a poster saying, "Veteran hospitals violate our rights." Another man in a beige trench coat tramped nearby with a sign reading, "Religion = Tyranny." Ruth couldn't imagine people harboring such beliefs that were so far away from the truth she felt in her heart. And there was poor Melissa seeing the jaded side of society. She grabbed her daughter's hand to pull her away from them and toward the safety of the hospital.

They scooted down the main hallway and stepped into the administrator's office. A man in a suit wearing horn-rimmed glasses was threatening to file a class action lawsuit against the hospital if the distribution of Christmas cards was not discontinued. He had thinning gray hair and a hunched back from leaning over a desk his entire life. This bookworm, who understood the theory of the law but not its practical effect on people, represented a national advocacy group that was Jonny-on-the-spot by arriving even before the news had been made public. Ruth could only shake her head. If someone were an atheist, this group would say, "Stand on that soap box over there and talk 24/7." But if someone actually believed in something by possessing a strong religious or moral belief, then this group could come up with a thousand reasons why that person should not be allowed to speak. And that was what this man was saying right now to Ms. Timmons, the chief administrator.

"We must remove her daughter from this building immediately," stated the man. "And her mother's actions should be monitored around the clock."

"I'm sorry," said Ruth. "I didn't think the cards would harm anyone. This country has *In God We Trust* printed on our money. It's a phrase taken from *The Star Spangled Banner.* Doesn't that show what most citizens want?"

"You are violating our rights," seethed the man.

"I must discuss this issue with Mr. Watkins further," said Ms. Timmons, who had a tired look on her face as though she had seen it all before. "Then I will decide what course of action the hospital will take."

Ruth turned to another man who sat in the corner and remained silent. His face had a serene glow and his hands were folded in his lap. She asked, "Don't I have any legal rights?"

"I wouldn't know anything about that," said the man.

"So you just represent the hospital?"

"I would like to think I represent everybody," he said. "My name is Luke. I'm the chaplain."

"The chaplain?"

The man lifted the lapel of his coat, unbuttoned his shirt, and pulled out a silver crucifix from underneath his T-shirt so Ruth could take a peek, then covered it quickly. He said, "Please follow me. We can discuss this in the chapel."

Luke led Ruth and Melissa through the hospital's main hallway toward the front entrance, then veered off to a side room with a plain wood door. The minister unlocked the door and flipped on the light. They strolled inside. Before Ruth could say anything, he locked the door behind them. Inside there were no pews, but folding chairs set up before a lectern. It could have been a small hall used by Toastmasters to teach people public speaking skills.

Luke trudged over to one side of the room and drew back a beige curtain to reveal a cross and altar, a white porcelain figurine of Mary, and a stained glass representation of a dove and rainbow. The minister admitted, "I have never shown these objects to anyone. It is against the regulations in the hospital's handbook."

"Not even to your congregation?" asked Ruth. "To the wounded soldiers?"

"Not even to them," he mumbled. "It is forbidden."

They stood toe to toe with their heads tilting forward.

"Mommy," shrieked Melissa, "why are you whispering?"

Ruth realized that this is what "free speech" had become. Whether you talked about a police-involved shooting, the going-ons in a foreign country, or cultural differences among U.S. citizens, it must be hush-hush. You had to lean close together like a couple about to step out onto a dance floor or find a secluded place to talk. So there they were: locked in a room and whispering so even poor Melissa could not overhear what they were saying.

Ruth drove home without saying a word. That evening she noticed dark bags under her eyes and a few strands of gray in her auburn hair, which she plucked out with tweezers. She clanged pots and pans and banged cabinets while cooking dinner, but couldn't help it.

During dinner her daughter said, "Mom, I'm sure it's not that bad."

"It is that bad," she replied.

After dinner Ruth sat in the kitchen and got comfort by reading inspiring verses in the Book. So she had to leave Melissa all alone in the living room watching television.

The next morning snow fell throughout the area, closing schools. Ruth planned to spend her day off doing stuff with her daughter. Then she was called in to work. Even though she might have to turn over her employee badge, she took Melissa with her. She couldn't afford day care. She buckled her daughter into the SUV and drove to the hospital through the mush on the roads. Snowflakes swirled about as they plodded through the parking lot toward the hospital's main entrance.

A few atheists still marched in front of the building, but on the other side of the entrance a dozen religious protesters treaded in an oval, challenging the others. An African-American woman chanted in a sing-song voice, "The end of the world is nigh…The end of the world is nigh." A serious looking white fellow kept shouting, "Gideon will slay the foes of our Lord," while toting a sign with a drawing of a vengeful soldier carrying a sword and trumpet. An older fellow with stringy gray hair and the ragged clothes of a hermit read aloud from a King James Bible reminiscent of an ancient prophet. Several chubby middle-aged men huffed and puffed while carrying around a twelve-foot long cross with a six-foot span, which had nails hammered in place of the hands and feet. And a dumpy middle-aged white woman in a plain coat carried around a mason jar full of blood while crying out, "The blood of the lamb will save your soul." Even though it probably contained animal blood, the sight made Ruth gag.

"Mom, who are these people?" asked Melissa.

"They're certainly not from our church," stated Ruth. "We share our message by telling stories about Jesus and beaming with an inner joy."

The news of the Christmas card confiscation had spread like wildfire through social media and now every oddball in the Mid-Atlantic region had shown up.

Ruth realized that if you believe in doubling the minimum wage, social programs for everybody, sanctuary cities to protect Latin American aliens, and that religion has no place in society, then you are allowed to speak. Conversely, if you believe corporations should pay no taxes, major social programs such as health care must be abolished, a wall should be built along the Mexican border to stop illegal immigrants, and that religious piety could be mandated, you are also allowed to speak. But if you are in the great middle - that 75 percent of the population which has a mix of opinions - then you have no rights of free speech. That explained why the national newscasts featured weather reports and "Person of the Day" stories during each daily broadcast because of the self-imposed censorship brought about by political correctness.

She spotted several vans with 4-foot antennas on top their roofs parked nearby. Local- beat reporters stood close to cameras, yakking to an audience impatient for something to happen. Bystanders milled about recording everything on their cell phones: close-ups of protesters on both sides, police leaning against their patrol cars, and visitors and staff flowing in and out the hospital doors. They were waiting for tempers to flare and a scuffle that could be broadcast on the news to millions of viewers.

When Ruth and her daughter entered the administrator's office, Ms. Timmons was pacing back and forth while Ms. Bludgeon, who had a scowl on her face as though she was the Grim Reaper for good works, sat nearby. Ms. Timmons declared, "There you are. We need to talk."

"I'm sorry," gasped Ruth. "My daughter didn't understand what she was doing. I made a mistake by letting her in here."

"It's too late for that," stated Ms. Timmons. "We got a mess on our hands. Why did you tell your church?"

"I don't know any of those people out there," said Ruth. Then she decided to speak up because she was concerned about the legacy she was leaving her daughter, "All I can tell you is this: A lot of people talk about *free speech*, but how many can live it? How many citizens would lose their jobs or be vilified on social media if they spoke freely? So those protesters are marching to get our constitutional rights back, as crazy as that seems."

"First, your daughter upset our patients with those cards," insisted Ms. Bludgeon. "Then you instigated a massive protest by contacting your church."

"Why don't we ask them?" asked Melissa.

"A bunch of hooligans carrying around signs and chanting slogans?" scoffed Ms. Timmons. "If we open our door to them, they might conduct a massive sit-in. We'll never be able to get rid of them."

"We should request that the police blast them with a water cannon," stated Ms. Bludgeon. "That would clean them off and send a message at the same time."

"It's okay if they support your side," huffed Ruth, "but if they support the other side then they are awful people or lunatics."

"Mom, not them," said Melissa. "The soldiers."

"What do they have to do with this?" asked Ms. Timmons. "They didn't craft the regulations we have to abide by."

"It's their lives we're talking about," said Ruth.

They trudged down the hallway to D Ward past employees and visitors who strolled by. Three-foot robots, delivering medicine from the pharmacy to nurses' stations throughout the hospital, rolled along the tile floor with a whining sound. Ruth wondered whether human beings were destined to live their lives like those desensitized machines.

When they entered D Ward, Sergeant Knox yelped, "Hey, little girl, you got a whole platoon with you."

"We're here on hospital business," stated Ms. Timmons. "I understand that your rehab was set back because of the Christmas card incident earlier this week."

"I'm ready for P.T!" boasted the sergeant. "Don't say that Henry Knox isn't willing to do his duty. I was just babying myself for a while. I went through basic training so I know what it will take to learn how to walk again with a prosthesis."

"I'm not bothered by it," stated Private Epstein. "Her Hanukah card gave me something positive to think about."

"I'm not upset either," piped up Chavez, who was getting a little color in his face. "There's a place for this," he pointed to the Purple Heart, "and a place for that."

"Very well," said Ms. Timmons. "We'll give back the cards for one day. I will invite the leader of the faith coalition inside to see for himself. Tomorrow we will officially enforce the hospital's regulations. If anyone talks to the media, they will be terminated."

"Our lips are sealed," said Ruth.

"I will be back at midnight," stated Ms. Bludgeon, "to confiscate the contraband."

The officials left the ward. Melissa and her mom redistributed the holiday cards. The sergeant ate a big bowl of chocolate chip ice cream and scheduled his first P.T. session for the following morning. Private Epstein planned to make his Hanukkah house decorations bigger than any other on the East Coast. And Chavez set the card with the yellow ribbon on a nightstand nearby. He reminisced about his family celebrations in Austin and had a vision of what the mesquite bush, ringed with yellow ribbons, looked like. It gave him the courage to Skype his wife. He set a laptop on the food tray fastened to his bed and propped himself up with pillows. As the connection was going through with high-toned beeps, static, and fuzzy visual images; he took a deep breath. Then the picture came through crystal clear. His wife sat before him with tan highlights in her dark hair that brought out the color of her eyes. "Isabel, you look beautiful," he blurted. "I miss you, baby."

"I miss you too," she replied with yearning in her voice. "Where are you?"

"I'm still in the hospital. I'll be here at least another month."

"I can't wait for you to get home," she said. "I want to squeeze you."

"My hug might not be the same."

"I've talked to the doctors," she stated. "I'll take you any way you are. You know how I feel."

He gazed into her olive eyes and proclaimed, "I love you." He reached out with his remaining hand and pressed his fingers against the glass of the laptop.

She did the same and pressed her fingertips against the screen.

They tried to touch even though they were separated by 1,500 miles.

Patrick's Christmas Surprise

With his short red whiskers fashioned into a goatee and a buckskin coat that he had won in a raffle wrapped around his stocky shoulders, Patrick could be mistaken for a mountain man. So when he and his kid brother stumbled through the woods onto the trail, they didn't look unusual at all. They saw a couple hikers taking a break about 30 yards away. Those guys had bandanas tied around their heads and wore plaid shirts. One came over and asked, "How can we get back to the parking lot?"

Patrick wanted to tell him to get lost, but didn't want to blow his cover. Stealing a pine tree the week before Christmas could get you thrown in jail. "Keep on this trail to the junction, then go right."

"Thanks, friend."

The hikers swung their knapsacks onto their backs and disappeared down the dirt path.

His kid brother asked, "You know where they're going?"

"No."

"Why didn't you tell them where the road was?"

"Don't be a fool."

He and Jesse climbed the hill as it flattened out into a plateau. Wind swept through a grove of pine trees making the trunks creak and the branches sway and clack against each other. Patrick stopped and looked up at a white pine about 20 feet tall. "Mary will like this one. She's been yapping about how she wants a real tree this year."

Jesse scanned the woods in both directions. His face and nose were as narrow as a fox, but he had none of the cunning or daring of that animal. "I don't know if we should do this."

"It's too late to get cold feet. We're already here."

"I can't do it."

Patrick knew he had to spur his kid brother on. "You pay taxes don't you?"

"Yeah, but..."

"We're getting back our tax money."

Patrick dug the axe deep into the trunk. The solid sensation of striking an object felt good. He did it again and again, developing a rhythm in his swing. Wood chips flew in the air and scattered on the ground. After he had built up a sweat and his arms had become sore, a large V was sliced into the trunk. "Come on, Jesse. Your turn." He gave the axe to his kid brother.

"Better be nobody coming," mumbled Jesse.

"Ain't nobody coming. I'm watching out."

Jesse began whacking the tree. The thudding sound echoed off other trees. When he got tired, he handed the axe back. Now there was a V on both sides of the trunk.

Patrick knew a couple more swings would bring it down. Every time he whacked the tree, the axe vibrated. Both of his hands became numb. A *crack* sounded and the tree tumbled down, landing with a crash.

They grabbed several branches near the base of the trunk and hauled it along the ground across the plateau. A sign posted on another tree read, *No Hunting*. Patrick stopped and laughed. "It doesn't say nothing about chopping down trees." They dragged the tree over the dirt path, brushing up a swirl of dirt, down a hill and through the stream, up a little ravine, and out to the road where his pickup was parked.

They had trouble fitting the tree into the bed of the pickup because of its bulk. The top stuck out over the hood farther than the foremast of a ship and branches hung over the doors. Even though Patrick slowed the pickup to 30 miles per hour, they had to roll down the windows and hold on to keep it from sailing away. He glanced into the rearview mirror and saw a state trooper tailing him. "Smokie's got a bead on us?"

"He knows about the tree," warned Jesse. "He's going to arrest us."

"He doesn't know nothing."

The siren wailed and the lights flashed on the trooper's car.

That's all he needed, thought Patrick. He was trying to save money so he could buy a big screen television for himself. He was planning to go down to Best Buy the day after Christmas and get one on sale. Now this jerk was going to ruin it by giving him a hundred dollar ticket for who knows what.

He pulled over.

The trooper got out of his car and trudged toward them.

"He's going to see the axe marks," muttered his kid brother through clattering teeth. "He'll figure out we raided the state forest."

Patrick grabbed Jesse's quivering arm. "Calm down! He ain't going to figure nothing. Let me do the talking."

The trooper peered through the window. "Looks like you got a big one."

"Yeah, officer," said Patrick. "I want to surprise my wife."

"Let me tell you something. A tree this size would surprise anybody. And it smells so fresh." His nose whistled as he inhaled the sweet scent. "Where did you get it?"

"Back in town."

"In town?"

"Yeah, at the lot by the gas station."

"It's hard to believe that old man would be peddling trees this big."

"He is. But we don't have no trouble seeing out the back window."

"That's not why I stopped you. You were weaving back and forth on the road. Can I see your driver's license?"

"Sure." Patrick pulled out his wallet and thumbed through it slowly so he could come up with a sob story. "We were going as slow as we could, officer. Like I said, I brought this tree for my wife because she just got out of the hospital. The doctors gave her chemo treatments for breast cancer. We wanted to get her something nice." He handed the officer his license.

The fellow grunted a few times, then tore off a copy of the ticket. "I'm giving you a warning this time. Be careful about switching lanes."

"You bet!"

Patrick sighed with relief. There was no fine on the ticket. He waited until the trooper pulled out and went ahead. Then he continued on home. The whole time he went through the list of accessories he would need to go with the big screen television: the remote control, the DVD machine, the subscription to over a hundred channels on cable…

His brother interrupted his thoughts, "I didn't know Mary had breast cancer."

"She doesn't. I made it up so that fool wouldn't give me a ticket with a fine. I'm saving a bundle on this Christmas tree and I'm getting my wife's gifts at a garage sale. I'm planning to buy a big screen TV for myself after the holiday."

"Oh, Patrick, sometimes I can't believe you're my brother. I got Bonnie everything she wanted for Christmas. I even got her a Dr. Phil doll. That's her favorite TV show. She records it every day on Tivo."

"Your wife must be a master puppeteer," chuckled Patrick. "Did she get her degree in that at Penn State?"

"She's not a puppeteer," objected Jesse. "I figure she can put the doll on her car's dashboard or on her desk at work."

"She's certainly pulling all of your strings," sneered Patrick.

He drove the rest on the way home without chatting to his brother. He couldn't believe what a chump he was. When he parked in the driveway, he ordered Jesse to help him carry their cargo inside. The branches scraped against the door frame when they squeezed the pine into the house. Some cones snapped off and rolled on the living room floor. The tree was too tall to stand upright so they cut off the top seven or eight feet, which made a nice little tree, itself. Jesse carted that outside and strapped it to the roof of his car. When they stood the tree up, they realized it was a behemoth. Green branches covered a quarter of the living room. When Patrick's wife saw it, her mouth dropped open and her eyes became as big as a child's on Christmas morning. Then she squinted and said, "There's something hanging underneath its boughs. They look like spider webs."

That was the first time Patrick saw what appeared to be globs of white cotton underneath the limbs of the tree. But he was proud of what he had done so he said, "Those aren't spider webs. That's Spanish moss."

"Spanish moss on trees up here? I thought that stuff only grows in the swamps of Louisiana?"

"It grows up here too. You can see for yourself."

She moved forward to conduct a closer inspection, but he met her with a warm hug that made her get lost in the moment. He wanted to keep the tree-snatching top secret.

They draped a string of colored lights around the pine and bought a box of white tinsel at the store. When they layered the tree, the tinsel blended in with the *Spanish moss* to look like snow hanging from its branches.

They brought each other presents, gift-wrapped the items, and put them under the tree. The heat in the living room made the sap ooze out and spread the fresh pine scent everywhere. His wife's face was framed by brunette hair and her eyes shined as bright as turquoise stones. She puckered her lips and pecked his cheek. Then she announced her verdict, "The tree is perfect."

On Christmas morning Patrick heard his dog whimpering outside the bedroom door. When he opened it, the dog rushed inside and trembled. "What's wrong, boy?" He strolled down the hall and spotted what appeared to be a grasshopper hanging onto the wall, but it was longer and leaner. Almost three inches long. And it appeared to be praying. He rounded the corner and saw them: hundreds of praying mantis that had emerged from their nests and were now crawling on the branches of the tree, hanging upside down from the ceiling, burrowing into the furniture, and cartwheeling on the floor. His wife let loose a scream behind him. The dog went berserk, spinning in circles and barking. His wife's hand was shaking, "Get rid of them."

He scurried around the living room to pick them up. He stuffed some into a trash can, but couldn't catch them all. They were all over the place.

"Take the tree back and make them call an exterminator," demanded his wife.

"We can catch them."

"Patrick", she pronounced his name in a high tone, the way she always did when she was angry, "if you don't take this tree back and get rid of those bugs, I'm going to my mother's house."

"I can't."

"Why not? Who sold you this tree?"

"Me and Jesse cut it down in the state forest."

"Oh, Patrick, how could you?" She stomped back into the bedroom.

He fumbled through the phone book and dialed all the numbers listed, but only one exterminator was willing to come out on Christmas. And that guy was going to charge him triple the regular rate. He knew with the money spent on that, his bank account would be drained. He had to say goodbye to the big screen television and all the accessories. Why did he always have such bad luck?

The exterminator who showed up at the door was still groggy from a Christmas Eve party. He wore a gray uniform and carried a rectangular box marked by a skull & crossbones. He was at least six and a half feet tall with a bald dome, walrus mustache, and thick eyebrows. When Patrick let him inside the house, he couldn't help saying, "You look like someone I've seen before."

"Everybody says I look like Dr. Phil," replied the fellow. "Some people say I sound like him." He looked around the living room. "*Let's get real.* You have a problem with praying mantises. *We can't change the situation unless we acknowledge the facts.* They're everywhere."

"Thanks, for your candor." Patrick wanted to clobber him. That's all he needed: a comedian.

His wife tramped out of the bedroom carrying a suitcase.

"Where do you think you're going?' asked Patrick.

"To my mother's house."

He hurried over and grabbed one end. "No you're not."

"Yes, I am."

"No, you're not."

"Folks, please," pleaded the exterminator. "*You need a time out.* Go sit in your kitchen and wait until I'm done."

"If you say so," said Mary curtly. "Would you like some coffee?"

"With cream, ma'am," he nodded.

Patrick followed his wife into the kitchen. They sat at the table without looking at each other. An eternity passed until the exterminator came in. He declared, "I put out several bait traps." Sitting down, he reached for a pastry from a serving plate, "May I?"

"Help yourself," said Mary.

The exterminator tasted the pastry and smacked his lips," Mmm, this is delicious. What's in it?"

"Raspberry jam and cinnamon. It's a homemade recipe."

"They're quite good." He sipped his coffee. "Patrick, are you having any?"

"No, I'm not hungry."

"Patrick, if you paid more attention to your wife's jellyroll, you might get along better with her."

"You can say that again," she snapped.

"And you, ma'am, can I ask how long you have been married?"

"Eight years," she replied tartly.

"I'm sure within those eight years you got along with each other now and then," the man stated. "So isn't this argument you're having a bit silly?"

"We do get along," blurted out Patrick. "I'm still in love with her."

"What did you say?" asked Mary, not sure she had heard him right.

Patrick peered into his wife's eyes and crooned, "I love you."

"That's the first time you said that in months!"

While the exterminator munched on the pastry and slurped coffee, Patrick and his wife couldn't stop glancing at each other. The man said, "Well, let's go out and take a look."

They moseyed into the living room and saw that most of the praying mantises had migrated into the bait boxes. "I'll take these to a plant nursery," explained the exterminator. "The caretaker can always use more insect-control specialists."

When he left, Patrick and Mary sat on the sofa.

"I'm sorry about what happened," said Patrick. "We can go into town and get a new Christmas tree if you want."

"That's okay, honey." She hugged him. "One surprise is enough for this year."

59667271R00075

Made in the USA
Charleston, SC
09 August 2016